Rebecca O'Connor's first collection of poetry *We'll Sing Blackbird* was shortlisted for the Shine Strong Award. Her writing has appeared in the *Guardian*, the *Spectator*, *Poetry Review* and elsewhere. She was a writer in residence at The Wordsworth Trust and is a recipient of the Geoffrey Dearmer Prize. She is co-founder and publisher of *The Moth* magazine. She lives in County Cavan, Ireland. *He Is Mine and I Have No Other* is her first novel.

@RebeccaMoth | themothmagazine.com

'Vividly calls up the atmosphere of small-town life, I could positively feel the damp mistiness of it on my skin'
Sophie Mackintosh, Booker-longlisted author of *The Water Cure*

'This is both a love story and, in a sense, a ghost story. It is a small, self-contained thing, spare and unembellished in its prose style . . . This extreme lightness of touch gives *He Is Mine and I Have No Other* a certain elegiac grace'
Irish Times

'Rebecca O'Connor captures vividly the small triumphs and catastrophes of being a teenage girl in rural Ireland, but in the further darkness to which she reaches is a truth for all generations'
Belinda McKeon, author of *Solace*

'Captures, with uncanny precision, the sheer ferociousness of teenage desire'
Irish Independent on Sunday

'Rebecca O'Connor's debut novel is vivid, authentic and compelling and may be the truest depiction of Irish rural girlhood since Edna O'Brien's *Girl With Green Eyes*. For that it is, and a lot more besides. What a treat it is to be introduced to such a genuine, compassionately humorous and profoundly tender voice'
Patrick McCabe, Booker-shortlisted author of *Breakfast on Pluto*

HE IS MINE AND I HAVE NO OTHER

REBECCA O'CONNOR

CANONGATE

This paperback edition published in 2019 by Canongate Books

First published in Great Britain in 2018 by Canongate Books Ltd,
14 High Street, Edinburgh EHI ITE

canongate.co.uk

I

The lines from 'Bluebells for Love' by Patrick Kavanagh are reprinted from
Collected Poems, edited by Antoinette Quinn (Allen Lane, 2004), by kind
permission of the Trustees of the Estate of the late Katherine B. Kavanagh,
through the Jonathan Williams Literary Agency.

British Library Cataloguing-in-Publication Data
A catalogue record for this book is available on
request from the British Library

ISBN 978 I 78689 262 I

Typeset in Centaur MT by Palimpsest Book Production Ltd,
Falkirk, Stirlingshire

Printed and bound in Great Britain by Clays Ltd, Elcograf S.p.A.

For my family

CR

He used to walk by our house every day at the same time, up past Molly's lane to the cemetery. No one took any notice of him so I didn't much either.

I went up there most days after school. It isn't far – about two minutes up the road, past a derelict cottage where wrens nest and tufted sedge grows out the windows. Past a car park, big enough for twenty or thirty cars. They parked right down by our house, in on the grass verge, for the bigger funerals. There were people who went to every funeral in the parish – the same familiar faces time and again, quietly chatting to one another as they strolled behind the hearse.

But he wasn't one of those.

I thought I knew the place like the back of my hand – the stories behind certain graves, like the orphans who'd died in the fire in town all piled in together, thirty-five of them, without names. And next to them two separate graves for the nuns. Little framed ghosts in their Holy Communion outfits with their jaundiced, freckled faces. Names worn away, railinged plots with whitethorn and wild rose, black-flecked marble, old plastic wreathes with moulding notes of love and condolence.

It's on a steep hill that leads down to the main road. At the top of the hill is a large stone cross on a block of slate. High black brambles behind that, thick with blackberries in late September, and behind those, fields for pasture. The prettiest plots are up there still, blanketed in snowdrops, and early spring primroses, and bluebells in May.

It's always cold, even in summer. The wind feels like it comes from off the dark surfaces of the lakes.

I imagined sometimes I could see the sea off in the distance, though the coast is over a hundred miles away.

An ink-dark line of yew trees runs down on the left, along the path from the car park. Down the middle of the cemetery is an unsheltered shale path; and a smaller muddy track, seamed with dock leaves and grass, cuts to the right, through the older part. I convinced myself they were splints of bone and teeth I could feel through the rubber soles of my shoes – small as chicken bones, some of them, like those of children's hands or feet.

A lone farmhouse, stuck to the top of a field beyond the road, used to offer the only glimmer of light between there and the next town over.

The first time I noticed him was one of those evenings that sucks the light slowly out of things. He was off in the far corner, almost blotted out by the shadow of the trees.

I sat still as anything beneath the stone cross, my knees pulled up to my chest, watching him, waiting for him to leave, but at the same time not wanting him to. He stood there for what seemed an age, his figure elongating, expanding in the darkness. Then he turned, scraping the heels of his shoes on the gravel, and walked towards the gate. No sign of the cross. No genuflection.

I was frightened of him in a way – of his grief, his loneliness. He looked like the loneliest person on earth just then. I imagined he was the type of boy who wondered about things, as I did, who broke his heart wondering about things. Who felt inexplicably lonely hearing voices in the next room, or cattle off in the distance, or the sound of tyres on the driveway.

CR

I remember that evening. It was dark by the time I got back from the cemetery. The white paintwork of the house was luminescent under a full white moon. I remember the sound of my feet crunching on the gravel. I remember it because it was the only thing I could hear besides the blood gushing in my ears. That particular evening the lawn looked like a sheet of pale green glass. And I could feel eyes on me as I passed the laurel hedge separating our house from the neighbours.

The garden at the back was pitch-black. I could just make out the frosty tufts of grass glinting in the light from the porch. The swing creaked slowly from side to side, the blue twine gnawing into the branch's old bark. If you swung high enough on the seat you could touch the lowest branches with your feet and see right out over the wooden gate onto fields, and to the river, which had burst its banks that winter. I tried not to look down, walking a tightrope of light from the porch, concentrating hard on my steps, and on the footsteps behind me of those little orphan girls in their white dresses, charred black at the hem.

Gran was sitting alone in the dark in the living room, her left hand slack on her lap, her head slumped to the side. The stroke three years earlier had left her with the notion that that hand was not her own, but my dead grandfather's.

Lazy Bones, she called him. She was forever complaining about his nails that dug into her while she slept, leaving sores on her belly and hips that Mam would have to clean and bandage.

An empty sherry glass sat on the nest of tables beside her, the half-empty bottle underneath. Blue was sleeping fitfully by her feet. I switched on the light and pulled an armchair towards the fire, close to hers. She woke with a jolt.

'Switch over if you like, love,' she said. 'I'm not watching this.'

But I couldn't sit still. 'I'll make you a cup of tea, Gran,' I said.

She patted her hand and said one for her and one for Lazy Bones please.

'Sure you can share,' I said, but she didn't seem to hear me.

The kettle was still warm. I stood looking at my reflection in the dark window pane as I waited for the water to boil. I tried to look through the glass but couldn't make anything out. There wasn't a sound from outside. No wind. The cows had moved off to the hollow corner of the field, furthest from the house.

That boy walking home in the dark. He wouldn't be scared of the dark as I was. He'd cock his ear to the animal sounds, turn towards the sudden beams of car lights, pulling himself slowly onto the mucky verge and gingerly stepping back onto the glistening surface of the road once all was quiet. It was difficult to imagine what that boy might be thinking as he walked home. And wrong for him to be spending his evenings as he was. That's what I thought as I let the tea bags in the pot brew to a dark pulp.

Gran liked her tea sugary – three, four spoons sometimes. I made it extra sweet for her.

She'd slouched further into her chair. I set down her tea and tugged at the pillow at the base of her back.

'Why do nails grow on dead people?' she asked, clicking the nails on her left hand. I wasn't sure if it was me she was talking to or herself.

'I put lots of sugar in your tea, Gran,' I said.

She needed to sleep, but I couldn't be doing with the removal of the false teeth, hauling her out of her clothes and into her nightie. So I ran up the stairs and turned on her electric blanket instead, then waited with her until Mam and Dad returned, flicking from channel to channel while she dropped in and out of sleep. Blue twitched her back leg as if she was trying to bury something.

CR

Mam and Dad seemed in no great hurry to put Gran to bed when they got in. Dad sat himself in his usual chair, straining slightly to one side towards the television, half listening to the news, half waiting to hear one of us speak – like he did when Mam had visitors over. Mam sank into the cushions of the settee. The veins on her hands, palm down on her belly, shone bluer than usual against her pale skin. The skin around her nails was all chewed.

'And where were you earlier, Lani?' she asked. 'I was looking for you. To see if you wanted to come to town with me.'

'I just went up the road . . .'

'What have I told you about going up there on your own, Lani?'

I didn't answer. I knew she wouldn't expect me to.

'Things are going to have to change in this house . . .'

She'd been threatening that as long as I could remember, but nothing ever did.

'Your father and I were over at the Reillys'. You know what they're like. You can't leave without taking a drink, and then you can't stay without having a second, and then they're highly insulted if you refuse a third.'

'Aye, it's vicious,' my father piped in.

Mam got up to put the kettle on and swayed suddenly to one side.

Dad hopped off his seat and went and took hold of her elbow. 'Take it easy, love.'

'I'm okay,' she said, flashing him an awful dirty look. 'I'm okay. Let go of me.'

That night I lay staring at the ceiling, listening to the clatter of dishes in the kitchen, then the sound of Mam cajoling Gran and Lazy Bones up the stairs to bed, followed by their plodding steps.

That room of Gran's was where I'd go to get away. All her things – the caked make-up in her pearly white vanity case, its gold-plated clasp rusted and broken; the crystal jewel box stuffed with cameo brooches and rings, bent kirby grips. Drawers filled with thread spools, dented snuff boxes, hair nets, baubles, perfumed powder puffs, old letters and postcards from Bettystown and Lourdes. A creased photograph of her other daughter, the one in England, 'Celia, aged nine' written on the back. Earnest-looking. And skinny as anything. It was the same one Gran had had at her house, before she got ill.

The kitchen in that house had always smelled faintly of

gas and burned sausages, and the cutlery was spotted brown with rust. And in the living room she'd have small heavy-bottomed glasses of whiskey and ginger for adult guests, red lemonade for me and the neighbours' children. And this girl who was my auntie, who I never met, peering down at me from the mantelpiece.

There was a hatch between the kitchen and the living room. I loved to pass things through that hatch, shutting the doors, opening them again. It's funny how I can remember those doors more clearly than most things – the oily feel of the paint, the slight jamming on the sill, the way the light was shut out so suddenly, or let in on a bright day.

It had been near a lake, that house. Next to a jetty that I remember sitting on, watching the coots murder each other.

There was a silver-framed picture of Gran in front of the three-way mirror of her dressing table, propped against the jewel case. She must have been only my age. She looked so different, her elbows perched on a card table, her head resting on her hands. Eyes dark as raisins, dark hair, straight mouth determined to give nothing away. I liked the company of this young girl. And when Gran wasn't there these things were all mine. I could sit before my reflections, soaking in the musty smells and the view through the window over the fields at the back of the house.

I couldn't sleep that night, couldn't think of anything else but that boy. I didn't want to think of anything else.

It was only the next morning that I finally drifted off,

dreaming I was on the swing in the back garden, swinging right over the river, my feet bare, my hands outstretched, the air filled with white flowers, and the sweet, buttery smell of whin. I looked down and saw that the seat was gone, the rope was gone, and I was floating – right over the river and into the fields beyond the house.

My skin was goose-fleshed when Dad called me for school, as if the blood had curdled right up to the surface.

'Lani, would you ever eat with your mouth closed?' Mam pleaded with me at the breakfast table, her breasts slumped low in her flowery dressing gown, hands cradling a mug of tea.

I burned my fingers uncapping my boiled egg, gave Mam my upturned empty, like I always did. She ran her fingers absentmindedly round the rim of her mug.

The sun bounced off every surface. It was the wrong way round somehow. I felt like it should be dark. I had a fondness for the darkness just then, I can't explain it.

It was better when I stepped outside and felt the prickling of the cold at the back of my nose and throat, the frost tightening the skin around my shins, my wrists, the air lifting me out of myself. Dad revved the car up the driveway. The engine stalled, the car rolled back a little, then jolted to a stop.

'Is Mam okay?' I asked.

'She wasn't feeling too hot last night, love, but she'll be grand . . . Probably one too many egg sandwiches over the way.'

Mam was never ill, except when she'd been ill with me. But that was different. She couldn't hold anything down for months. Then once she got me out of her *I* couldn't hold anything down for months. I was a great spitter and dribbler. So she'd tell me – and of how she'd piled on the pounds, and had to spend the rest of her life weight-watching. Every pound and ounce she'd watch. She'd eat nothing but banana sandwiches for lunch until she couldn't look at another banana, then nothing but baked potatoes and beans, then Ryvita and cottage cheese, and on it went. Mondays, Wednesdays and Fridays she'd speed-walk around the hospital grounds with Mary Reilly from over the road, or with one of the ladies from the office. There was a bit of a craze in town for speed-walking. You'd never see a jogger or a stroller – just groups of middle-aged women swinging their arms and waddling their arses round certain well-worn routes. You'd hear them coming before you'd see them, the swish of their shiny tracksuits. Then heading down to Weight Watchers in the town hall every week to be weighed in front of everyone, like the prize pikes you'd see in the local paper.

Anyway, she was fine, Dad said. I thought nothing more of it, is the truth. I'd other things to be thinking about. All those hours spent the night before trying to conjure up this boy. A boy I'd only ever seen far off and in the evening when the light was poor. He was from the school down the road: he wore the uniform of dark grey trousers, white shirt, navy tie, grey jumper. He was a boarder, for sure – not just because he was always in uniform, but because no one around our neck of the woods seemed to know *who* he was. I'd surely have heard one of the neighbours mention him, if only to say they'd offered young so-and-so a lift, or they'd seen young so-and-so on the road.

I was trying to put him together in my mind's eye – tall, hair dark brown, skin pale – but I was at a loss as to the shape of his hands or the colour of his eyes. Or to what it was had changed about him or me that night that I could never be the same.

CR

Dad dropped me at the bottom of the laneway up to school that morning. Usually he'd drop me right outside the front door but we were running late. I'd spent ages in the bathroom staring into my eyes, the size of my pupils: they were that dilated the blue of the iris was almost invisible.

There were dozens of girls pouring out of school buses, smoking inside the front gates, their shoes scuffed white, skirts rolled up round their thighs. There were boys on the buses too, which made the skin on my face and neck taut and hot, even though I knew for sure there were none of them I'd like. They were all smaller than me, for one thing. And they smelled, most of those boys. They smelled like they had dirty things on their minds.

I went round where the cars were meant to go, rather than the path at the side, and slipped crossing the cattle grid, grazing the palms of my hands on the pebbledash of the gate pillar. My whole body burned with embarrassment.

I wanted to scramble through the ditch and run through as many icy fields as it would take for me to feel cold and in control again – dozens of icy fields, so that I could feel the wet soaking into my wool tights. But I just squeezed the strap of my school bag with both hands, digging my nails into my palms, and walked as fast as I could without looking, like I wanted to disappear. It wasn't that I was worried what they thought of me, but that they would see me at all, look at me, watch me. That's what I hated more than anything.

On up past the rhododendrons, covered in a mint frost, past the woods on the right, past the nuns' plot of vegetables, the gardener spreading pot-ash. I could feel the cold trickling down my neck and down my spine. Past the statue of the Virgin Mary and child. The redness fading from my cheeks. Sister Rosario off in the distance. Only her legs, in their skin-coloured nylons, seemed to be moving. The rest of her covered in a dark grey habit the colour of her eyes. Her tiny hands folded under the heavy sleeves. She nodded and smiled at me, and I felt better for seeing her.

I said, 'Hello, Sister,' in a voice that wasn't really my own.

⚭

First class that morning was pastoral care.

'And Lani, would you like to draw around Josephine please?' says Sister Anne, handing me a lump of blue chalk.

I went beetroot and nearly tripped over myself. Josephine was lying on a large sheet of paper in the middle of the floor, her scrawny body twitching with embarrassment. The desks and chairs were stacked up against the walls, and the rest of the girls standing around her. I crouched down on my hunkers first, then onto my knees, and drew a vague outline. I didn't want to have to touch any part of her, not even her clothes – especially not in front of all those other girls. I didn't even know what we were supposed to be doing, but I'd have looked stupid if I asked then.

'You can get up now, Josephine,' Sister Anne shrilled when I'd finished.

Josephine was given a hand up by one of the girls. Some of the others sniggered into their sleeves. She left a blurred white shadow on the ground behind her. It made it look like she was fat.

'Now, we need a name for her. What will we call her?'

Betty, someone said, then Genevieve, Dolores – until finally Mar shouted 'Ezmerelda!' and everyone turned to look at her. She grinned at me. All heads nodded eagerly: Ezmerelda it was. Sister Anne was working us into a right frenzy. There was nothing we liked better than this sort of feckless exercise, a good forty-five minutes of light relief from the deathly boredom of maths or Irish.

I tried to ignore Josephine, but felt compelled to watch her all the same. I had that exact feeling I'd had in primary school when we were all paraded in our underwear in front of the district nurse. The boys had to show the nurse inside their pants, so that she could make sure everything was in order. I remember feeling my nipples stiff as little apple pips through my cotton vest. Then the prick of the booster injection on my forearm.

One girl was called up to draw Ezmerelda's face. She did so with such avid attention to detail that it got on Sister Anne's nerves.

'Now, Claire, you needn't worry too much. It doesn't have to be perfect. Just so we get an idea,' she said.

Then she took the blue chalk herself and went on: 'Now, where would I find the breasts?'

She scanned the room, and went back to Claire.

'Claire?'

Claire pointed.

'Yes, that's right. Very good. Silly question, I know!'

And she drew two little eggs, sunny side up. Claire blushed right to the roots of her hair, and so did Josephine.

Sister Anne outlined the arms and legs.

'And what do we find here?' she asked, pointing somewhere roughly around the armpit.

'Hair?' someone croaked, just as the silence was getting too much.

'*Yes*, that's right,' she said.

And she drew a little bush either side of each sunny egg.

And on she went, until she got to the vagina, the womb, the fallopian tubes, which looked like a girl skipping, the way she drew them.

It turned out that this lesson was not about sex. We knew about that already. It was about the *smell* of the sex, and how important it was to wash and deodorise those areas where hair had recently sprouted. I wondered, as Sister Anne said the Hail Mary at the end of class, if she ever looked at herself, naked, after a bath.

Mar and I sat in the cloakroom at elevenses, as we always did.

'Well, what's the matter with you? I saw you moping up the lane this morning.'

'I was up half the night,' I mumbled, tearing the plastic wrapper on my snack bar with my teeth. Mar bit into her apple.

'Up half the night with what? Are you sick? What happened you?'

'Don't laugh, but I think I'm in love.'

'Ah, would you give over,' she said, roaring with laughter. Bits of apple and spittle flew out of her mouth.

I knew she'd react like this. It was a weekday: where on earth would I have seen or met a boy to fall in love with? I hadn't been near the shops. And there'd been no mention of him before. As far as she was concerned I had the hots for one of her neighbours, the one I'd played a game of pool with once in her garage.

He'd been going up to the graveyard for as long as I could remember, I told her, but only the night before had it suddenly occurred to me – like a flash of lightning, was what I said – that he was *the one*. I told her about the dream I'd had that morning. That seemed to convince her.

'So who is he?'

'He's a boarder up at St Colum's.'

'You don't even know his name? For fuck's sake.'

We took our pimply legs down from the bench opposite to let two girls pass, then slouched back down again, our heads sinking into dozens of maroon-coloured coats and blazers. Mar took another bite out of her apple. The bell rang.

'I suppose we'll see him at the Colum's disco anyway.'

'Do you think we'll be let go?'

'No,' she smiled, 'but so.'

There was a list of things to do stuck to one of the cupboards in the kitchen. A sure sign there was something wrong with Mam: she'd never written a list before in her life. She just got on and did things. There was no question of sitting about making notes.

I could hear her on the landing. She had the radio on.

'Why wouldn't I be?' she croaked when I asked her if she was okay, her head peering round the top of the stairs. She had that deranged look on her face she got after spending more time than is good for anyone ironing sheets and underpants. She was a little peaky-looking too.

'Are you feeling better?'

'*Me*? I'm fine. Why wouldn't I be?'

'Dad said you weren't feeling too well.'

'Jesus, that man can keep nothing to himself. I'm *fine*. I had the one glass of wine and it didn't agree with me is all.'

Blue was yelping to be let in. She must have heard me being dropped off at the gate from school. She'd stopped barking suddenly. Then there was a loud knock, and another – a thud. I found her ready to throw herself against the door for a third time when I went downstairs.

'You're weird, Blue,' I said, crouching down to pet her.

She looked up at me and wagged her tail, mouth hanging open for air, as if she'd run round the world to welcome me home. The fur on her belly and legs was soaking wet, and she was raring to jump up on me, her nails scratching the parquet floor. I turned and she followed, panting.

Mam was in the bathroom upstairs. I stood on the landing beside her ironing board, holding my breath, wondering if I should ask her again if she was okay. The iron was still hot. She'd put out clean linen for my bed.

'Mam, don't worry about changing my sheets. I'll do it myself.'

She didn't respond. I went and got the blow-dryer out from the drawer of her dressing table, plugged it in in my room, and pointed it at Blue. Her legs quivered.

'It's for your own good. If you want to come anywhere near me. You're soaking wet.'

Her hair was starting to whiten – around her mouth and eyes, and around the star-shaped patch on her breast. She was forty-nine in dog years – half my age if I were a dog. If I were a dog I might be dead, I was thinking.

Then I heard the click of the lock on the bathroom door and Mam's standing looking down at me and at Blue.

'Now what have I told you about blow-drying the dog in here? You've my heart broke.'

She had a thing about dog hairs getting into the carpet and onto my duvet and curtains.

'And that awful smell—'

Her eyes were bloodshot.

'For God's sake, Mam,' I said. I couldn't think what else to say, and I couldn't not say anything. I didn't want her noticing I'd seen how red her eyes were. 'There's no hairs . . .'

She turned abruptly and walked out, Blue skulking at her heels.

Gran was watching an old *World Series of Poker* video, with Lazy Bones tucked snugly under her right arm. It was raining. I could hear it thrumming on the windows. I glanced up at the road. No sign of him. It was a little early yet. The air was so heavy with rain I worried I might not see him if he passed by. Dad was out the back, breaking branches over his knee, setting another fire. I stood at the kitchen window and gazed out at him, wanting to cry. I wandered from room to room, avoiding going up to my own, where Mam was fussing over my unmade bed, the clothes on my floor, the dog hair, her eyes still sore-looking. Without bothering to change out of my school uniform as I usually would, I threw on one of Dad's old jackets and skulked off to the graveyard. I didn't turn to hear what Dad said as I passed him. I couldn't be sure, anyway, if it was me he was talking to or himself, as he often talked to himself, and I didn't want to have to explain to him where I was going at this time of night and in this kind of weather and with my school uniform still on me.

A drizzle of sweat had formed on my back and on my forehead before I'd even reached the top of the drive. I could feel my face reddening as I put my hand up to pull strands of hair away: they were sticking to my skin, catching at the corners of my mouth and in my eyelashes. There was no sign of anyone on the road. I turned up left to the graveyard, walking in on the grass verge. I waved at passing cars though I couldn't see the drivers' faces. Headlights were blurred in the rain. As I turned past the cottage and walked up through the side gate I realised I wasn't alone.

He was there. Earlier than he'd been the evening before, earlier than he should have been, standing in the same place, staring off into the distance. I went suddenly cold. I tried to get a good look at him, but it made me feel kind of dizzy, like I might faint. And the rain. And again we were too far apart for me to make out any detail.

He didn't seem to notice me. I kept walking uphill, fingers tearing at old bits of tissue and chewing-gum wrapper inside the pockets of Dad's coat. I could hear Blue panting behind me, which worried me for a moment – *he* might hear her too – but the noise from the rain on the trees would have drowned out any small sound. Blue ran ahead of me.

I felt so exposed up there – not just to the rain and the wind, but to him. I'm sure he'd seen me there before – he must have – but before it hadn't bothered me. I hadn't thought how unbearable it could be for his eyes to be on me, though it's what I wanted more than anything. I pulled the mac down below my backside, held it taut, and sat on the edge of the slimy slate beneath the stone cross, praying he wouldn't notice. Blue was sniffing around the headstones, sticking her nose into plastic wreathes, trying to bite blades of grass. She could smell herself on things. She chomped the air and sneezed. She was moving further and further away from me, down the path. Towards him.

Then he stood up and held his hand out to her, and I could just make out his voice calling to her, and him whistling. And my hearing seemed to go: there was a sudden hush in my ears like hailstones. I was burning hot, though my skin was stinging cold. The boy was down on his haunches then, and Blue clawing his knees. She only did that with people she knew.

I didn't dare look straight down at them. Instead I looked the other way, pretended to myself I was looking at something in the trees, resting my head in my blue hands in an effort to shield my face from him and cool my cheeks. I was sure my thoughts were there, clear as day, to be read. I couldn't just up and leave. I was stuck.

I don't know how long I was there but my hair was sopping, and I could feel the wet soak into my skirt, and I thought, all of a sudden, if I stayed a moment longer it would be too late. Too late for what, I didn't know. I drew myself up slowly, hands still in pockets, and sauntered back down the way I'd come, beneath the yew trees. I didn't once look over at him. My legs nearly went from under me a couple of times as I walked down the laneway and on to the road. And I didn't look back once to see if Blue would follow, though I heard her a few minutes later, just as I could see home.

The kitchen was warm with smells from the oven, and I felt ravenous with hunger. Mam was back to her cheery self, fanning the smoke from pork chops under the grill with a tea towel. There were spuds on the boil, and steam rising from other pots of vegetables. She smiled at me as I walked in.

'Look at you. You're soaked.'

She told me dinner would be five minutes, and didn't I have good timing, and would I call Dad. No word about where I'd been or what I'd been up to. The table was already set. Gran's beanbag tray was laid with cutlery and salt and pepper sachets. For some reason, since she'd come out of hospital, Gran preferred those sachets, even though they were obviously much more difficult for her to use. I went to the hall door and called Dad, listening for my own voice echoing.

'I think he might be outside still, love.'

'But it's dark outside. What's he *doing*?'

I was uncomfortable in my wet clothes, and irritated all of a sudden by Mam. And here was Blue, who'd just nearly given me heart failure, acting as if nothing had happened, the stupid dog.

I could just make out a tiny blotch of red where Dad's

fire had been as I stood at the back door, and the smell of damp burned wood, but no sign of him. I shouted into the darkness. His voice ghosted out from the shed, and a dull beam of light from his torch fell on the gravel. Blue ran out through my legs towards the shed, barking at him, then back at me, lingering halfway between us, unsure of what to do next. Dad appeared, patted her roughly on the head, and she dashed into the house ahead of him. His face was ruddy with the cold and his hands smeared with green and black mould and sap from the wood.

'You're to wash your hands before you come anywhere near the table,' Mam told him.

There was small talk over dinner that evening – about the Christmas holidays, and the new gravel the Reillys had bought for their driveway. Gran ate, as usual, in front of the television in the front room. I cleared the table afterwards and put the kettle on. Mam told me to get the chocolate Hobnobs out of the cupboard, like a good girl. We only ever had them when we had visitors.

'Now sit down, love,' she said, and told me, in a bit of a roundabout way, that she was going to have a baby.

I said nothing.

Mam was forty-four. That was way too old to be having babies as far as I was concerned. I suddenly felt a terrible itch at the back of the knees from the damp tights I had on me.

Dad said nothing.

The first thing I asked was 'How long?' I might as well have asked them right out when they'd last done it. It made me feel sick, talking about this here in our kitchen. After dinner. On a school night. They were still at it. At their age. Under this roof. While I lay innocently tucked up in bed. All the filthy details rushed into my head then: they mustn't have used a condom, or, worse than that, they *had* used one and it had come off or broken. My mind's eye was forced to zoom in to the moment of its removal from the penis. (I couldn't think of it as anything other than a 'penis'. The names the girls at school used seemed inappropriate.) I thought about gobbing on her.

'Baby's due tenth of May,' Mam said.

'Tenth of May, love,' Dad said.

He was turning one of Gran's sachets of salt over and over between his thumb and forefinger. It made a tiny swishing noise like surf.

I fucking heard you, I wanted to say. Shut your fucking mouth.

Then, to make things worse, they suggested that I move to the big room downstairs so that they could use my room as a nursery. I'd been in that room since I could remember. But that didn't seem to concern either one of them.

The whole time Mam was stroking my shoulder with one hand while her other lay protectively on her belly. It was too much. I tore out of the room and bolted myself into my bedroom for the rest of the night. They didn't follow me. They knew better than to do that.

That night I dreamed all the little orphan girls were living with us. Only there wasn't enough room in the house so I had to sleep outside in the shed. And I watched them through the kitchen window, all bawling and clawing at my mother for milk. And then I was watching myself watching them through the window and I woke up in a cold sweat.

Mar was warming herself on the classroom radiator, her skirt hoiked up just under her buttocks, her long skinny legs resting on the back of one of the plastic chairs.

'You look like shit.'

'Thanks.'

I couldn't tell her. I don't know why. I told her I hadn't slept.

'Thinking about your man again?' She wiggled her hips. 'Disco is on the twen-tee-fourth. I heard on the bus this morning.'

I felt a little faint with excitement.

Mar underlined 'come' in the last line of 'Sailing to Byzantium' in English class that morning – 'Of what is past, or passing, or to come' – and pushed her book in front of me. I didn't even laugh. Usually I would. Usually we'd both nearly choke laughing. But it just made me want to cry. And the words 'perne in a gyre' spinning round in my head.

After lunch we went out to the woods to collect specimens of moss and fern and suck insects into pooters. Beetles, mostly. And woodlice. I walked a little behind the rest of the class, the sleeves of my jumper pulled down over my hands. I had this weird feeling I was being watched, and even glanced quickly behind me a few times to make sure. The trees were bare; I could see right to the road; there wasn't a soul about. Not even a car passing. The sky was milky blue. It looked as though it might snow.

Soon the walls of my bedroom would be painted in pastel shades for the baby, and my bed replaced by a cot. And how was I going to convince Mam and Dad to let me go to this disco when they'd already said that I could only go out (maybe) during the holidays? What if I never got to meet this boy? I could hardly approach him in the cemetery. It had to be a slow set. Somewhere dark, crowded, noisy, so that he couldn't see or hear me too well. My mother was going to swell and give birth. I wouldn't be the only one anymore. I would have to look after it when they were too old. They were going to die.

Mar ran back and handed me a woodlouse in a jar. 'Here, you can look after this.'

'Great, thanks a bunch, Mar,' I said, putting a foot out to trip her up. At least I had her.

⚮

It was around that time that Celia's book appeared on Mam's bedside locker. Mam hadn't said a word about it. Mind you, I'd hardly spoken to her after she told me about the baby. But I was sure she wanted me to find it. I was always snooping around her room, trying on her clothes. Sometimes even Dad's clothes, I got so bored of my own. It was like when she left a copy of *What's Happening to Me?* in my room. She didn't say anything that time either.

She just waited.

I used to keep it under my mattress and take it out every night to look at the rude pictures of girls with varying sizes of boobs, and boys standing on diving boards trying to hide their erections. I never said anything to her about it. But then one day she just called me into her bedroom and read through it with me, very slowly. As if I couldn't read. She read it straight through from cover to cover, then asked me if I had any questions. I said 'No' and got off the bed as quick as I could and went outside in the garden to play.

I knew that Gran had had to give Celia up because she wasn't married. Mam and Uncle Patrick had had some kind of falling out over it. That was all I knew. If I ever asked Mam she'd just say, 'I'll tell you when you're older.' The book, which was called *The Little Ones*, was a black glossy hardback with a photograph on the front of a serious-looking little girl. She looked like she'd lost her mother, like I did once in the supermarket, only she'd lost her so long she'd given up bawling. It was inscribed inside 'To Deirdre. With love from your sister, Celia'. I didn't even know they were in touch. I couldn't think of Celia being a grown-up. She was just this wee girl on the mantelpiece, suspended in the past. The back stated simply that Celia lived in Oxford with her two cats. I remember that making me cringe, the idea that she was one of those smelly cat women. She probably had no children. Probably treated her cats like they were human.

The introduction was brief:

Industrial schools were commonplace in Ireland up until the latter half of the twentieth century. Poverty-stricken families, mainly, and unmarried women were compelled to send their children to these institutions. Tens of thousands of children, only a small proportion of whom were actually orphans, ended up in detention.

The schools were run by Catholic religious orders,

36

and were prevalent in cities and towns throughout the country. Contrary to popular belief they were not charitable but state-run organisations. The Department of Education provided a grant for each child committed by the courts. This institutionalised method of child-care was economically more viable than providing individual families with financial support. It also appeased the Catholic Church by allowing them to maintain a level of political power within the community.

One such school, established in 1869 and run by an enclosed order of nuns, was in operation for almost 100 years. What the girls suffered there is not unique. What is unique, however, is the way in which thirty-five of these girls so needlessly lost their lives.

On the night of 23 February 1943 a fire started in the laundry of the convent. As the fire intensified some girls tried to jump from the second-floor windows, while others were overcome by smoke or consumed by flames. The thirty-five girls who perished were buried in an unmarked grave.

What follows is a brief glimpse into the lives of these girls, a means of memorialising and remembering their all-too-short lives. Using what information I could glean about their backgrounds, their ages and the running of the school, through research and interviews with survivors, I have tried to give each girl a unique voice.

We need to be reminded not only of the systematic

abuse here and throughout the country, but of the fact that these girls were not simply numbers. They had names.

She had very good English, I remember thinking, probably because she lived in Oxford. The thought of those girls used to keep me awake when I was little. I couldn't have the curtains open, not even the tiniest bit, in case I caught sight of them at the window. And now I was afraid all over again, as if they would come for me in the night.

Denise, 12

I am number 17. That is not my age! It is the special number I was given when I first came here. Sometimes I forget that my name is Denise. My favourite thing is to make paper dolls and cover them in silver paper, which me and my friend Aisling get from the bin at school, from the townie girls' sweet wrappings. We tear the wrappings into wee jumpers and skirts and boots. At night we put the dolls in matchboxes to sleep. Aisling doesn't give hers any names even though I told her to. She says she can't think of any so she just gives them numbers too, like us.

When I grow up I am going to be a nun like Mother Assumpta, not like Mother Carmel. I pray every day, even when I'm not supposed to. Everyone has to line up and pray first thing in the morning, at six. I get up at five because I'm afraid of being hit and because I like to pray before everybody else. And then we wash and go to mass and have communion, and say 'Our Father' and sing 'Holy, Holy'. And I pray when I'm doing the scrubbing in the morning too, mostly the Hail Mary over and over until sometimes I start to get a bit dizzy and get the words mixed up. Then I feel bad for that and have to ask forgiveness. From God and from Our Lady.

I always bow my head when I say 'Jesus'.

My other favourite thing as well as my dolls is Christmas. On Christmas we get to eat meat and gravy. The ladies from the cathedral come in to serve us, the ones that don't have their own children. They're the same ones who stay with Father Fagan in the room behind the altar on Sundays and then come out to give us communion. They don't say very much. They're a bit like Aisling that way. Maybe she will be like one of those women when she grows up, and she'll see what's in that room at the back of the cathedral.

My worst thing is Jeyes Fluid. It's when the townies bring lice into class, and then we have to have our heads scrubbed with Jeyes until they're almost bleeding. Sometimes they *do* bleed. It stings like when you cut onions. I don't remember ever having lice before I came here. Mother Assumpta tells me I was six when I came. I don't remember. I don't have a birthday like the other girls. Mother Assumpta says we can celebrate my birthday as the day I came in here, June 21st. It's only pretend. We don't tell anyone else. Not even Aisling.

Just me and her. She gives me sweets in the laundry, which I'm not allowed to show to anyone. I won't tell anything. I'm a good girl.

Green and pink and yellow wrappers. I use them to make dresses. That's my other favourite thing! Aisling asks where did you get those and I tell her to keep her gob shut. She says the convent is a bad place but she's lying. I've already said three good things.

I must have had a father and a mother but no one seems to remember. It was like I was dropped from the sky by a stork, Mother says. But I wasn't a baby. I was six. How do they know what age I was? And why is it I can't remember anything?

CR

Mar and I talked about little else besides the disco – how we'd get there, what we'd wear, whether our hair would be up or down. No detail was too small. I stashed a couple of cans from the drinks cabinet under my bed. And Mar was going to steal some of her mother's fags. Buying cigarettes wasn't the easiest thing to do, as there was always a danger we wouldn't be served, or that somehow the news would get back to our parents. You couldn't do anything in this town.

We decided it best not to ask our parents if we could go. That would blow our chances altogether.

I didn't go near the graveyard. I didn't want to see the boy until the night of the disco. I couldn't bear to. And anyway I didn't want him thinking I was spying on him.

Mam didn't look so different then – maybe just as if she'd eaten a few too many custard creams, which she *had*, so most of the time I could convince myself that it was one of those phantom pregnancies, where women carry ghosts around in their bellies, or that really she was suffering from menopause, though I wasn't sure what that was.

I started to put things away in my new room – very slowly and reverentially to fold things into themselves. Nothing was ever so neat in my old room. My new room was bigger. It was colder too. One of the radiators was broken and the other one only half worked. Dad said he'd see to them but I knew he'd never get around to it. The walls were white rather than pink. And suddenly I seemed to have fewer things than before. They were stacked neatly against one wall in boxes. I put the few books, trinkets and cassettes I had onto the shelves above my new bed, and left the walls bare. I had all these posters rolled up, but I didn't know where to put them. Jim Morrison and Laura Palmer didn't look right on the new walls. The wardrobe was big enough almost that you could walk into it, and my clothes hung in it like dolls' clothes.

The long mirror opposite the bed frightened me: I could see things moving in it in the darkness. It didn't matter that I knew it was only my eyes playing tricks. If you looked at your own reflection by candlelight you'd see the devil looking back at you – that's what people used to say. It didn't have to be candlelight for me to be frightened out of my wits. Especially reading Celia's book. I turned the mirror against the wall some nights, but even then I imagined things crawling out of it.

Where before my only view had been of the sky and the

tops of the laurel bushes through a skylight, now I had the whole of the back garden. The window was long and narrow. It was strange to be able to see the ground: it made the room feel like a greenhouse, like I could step outside if I wanted to. The birds weren't as loud from here as they had been upstairs, but I could see more of them before it got dark. I could see the swing, too, and the light fading from the sky above the fields. I had my desk so that it was facing out onto all of this, and at first there were no curtains, only an old thin white sheet, so I was woken early every morning until I adjusted to the light, and my dreams adjusted with it. They became all bright and watery, like I was in a flotation tank or something, and I'd wake as easily as if I had just blinked, barely remembering what it was I had been dreaming about.

I watched out for him as often as I could, though I could hardly make out his shape in the dark. It was pitch-black most afternoons, arctic. And at night I'd lie awake, wondering why he went up there, who it was he went to see, feeling peculiarly out of kilter in my new bed. Disturbed in turn by the emptiness, the *lack*, and then by the overwhelming abundance of things: the baby, that boy, those little girls burning. Often I had to sleep with the light on to make sure a ghost of the boy wasn't in the room, visiting me as he visited that grave. I'd get a tight pain in my chest and find it hard to breathe. Other times I was glad of the darkness: it allowed me to wallow in unfinished thoughts of him, the half-remembered features. And sometimes I felt,

45

sinking my head into the pillow and burning a picture of him on the inside of my eyelids, that I could float off the bed if I put my mind to it.

Mar arrived over on the afternoon of the disco.

'And how are you, Mar? We haven't seen you in ages,' Mam beamed, turning from the sink to look at her, her yellow Marigolds dripping muddy water onto the kitchen floor. It was like she was making a special effort to behave as if nothing had changed since Mar's last visit.

'Ah, not too bad, Mrs Devine, not too bad,' Mar says, leaning on the counter in the kitchen all casual so as not to give Mam any idea we were up to anything.

'Is your mother well? I don't see her about much. Is she not working in Donoghue's anymore?'

'Oh, she's in grand form. She is, yeah – just Saturday now, though.'

Mar blushed. She didn't usually blush but she was in a right state that day, straining to hide her nerves.

I dragged her out of the room and into my new bedroom. Mam was smiling to herself as I turned to close the door behind me, and I could hear the slippery sound of the peeler on wet spud.

'What's happened to your old room?'

'Had to move out. Mam's having a baby and she wants to turn my room into a nursery.'

'Jesus. Fuck.'

'Yeah, I know.'

'Isn't she a bit old? When's she having it?'

'Way too bloody old. May.'

'Christ.'

'That's what I said.'

The rest of the day we spent between my room and the kitchen, gorging on yoghurts, chocolate bars, biscuits, crisps – anything we could find that took our fancy. I showed Mar *The Little Ones*, and told her Celia was my auntie and she told me to go away to fuck. We creeped ourselves out reading bits of it aloud. She gave Gran some funny looks later that evening when we were having supper and I kicked her under the table.

We were worried sick we'd be caught that night, or, even worse, we wouldn't have the nerve to go through with it at all. I told Mar every move I was going to make. I was going to walk up to him after the first slow song but before the second started (a small enough window but long enough to get in there before someone else). There was no way I was going to wait for him to ask me. What if he didn't? I mightn't be out again for months. I'd put my arms around his neck, he his hands around my waist, dance slowly – Mar and I practised in front of the long mirror – and stroll out casually into the dark. Mar herself was going to be whisked off her feet by some dashing stranger, though only after she'd witnessed *my* special moment. It would probably be the second slow set for her so she wouldn't have as much time to shift outside afterwards, but that was just the way of the world.

We'd told our parents we were going to Mona's to watch videos – meeting her at the chippie in town first, going to get some vids, then her dad would be picking us up. He'd drop us home later. Mona *did* exist. We just didn't have, or want, anything to do with her. Mam and Dad were having some of the neighbours over for cards and sandwiches: they'd all be well jarred by eleven or so, and we'd be back shortly afterwards. We'd never done a thing wrong before that night besides steal the odd smoke, which was hardly the crime of the century, so our parents had no reason to doubt a word we said.

Jeans, a T-shirt and a tatty old jumper was what we both had on, so that we wouldn't look conspicuous. I had mascara and some pink lipstick I'd stolen from Gran's room, and Mar had a blunt black eye pencil.

Dad dropped us off at the chippie, telling us to ring him if we needed a lift home later. I had sweaty palms.

We strolled casually in and stood motionless under the fluorescent light as we watched his car pull off. The couple sitting by the front window, tucking into chicken boxes, licked the greasy crumbs from their fingers. In between mouthfuls they'd glance out at the street, away from one another. The pimply young boy behind the counter didn't much care if we ordered or not. We headed straight for the ladies' loos. They smelled of stale piss and used tampons. We applied our make-up under a blinking light. Our hands were shaking. I didn't dare put too much on. I was shy of my own reflection. Mar circled her eyes, even pencilling along the fine layer just inside the lashes. She applied mascara with that pouting concentration I thought only mothers possessed. We bought two cans of Coke and walked the mile or so back towards my house, to the boys' school. If anyone we knew saw us we'd be in trouble, but we were willing to take the risk. We could always come up with some excuse, like Mona hadn't shown up, and we thought we'd just walk back to my place rather than drag Dad away from the neighbours and the cards.

We clung to one another as we walked up the dark muddy avenue, beneath the lonely cawing of crows in the trees. There was no moon that we could see. It was difficult to find our footing. We only had the faint light from the street lamps on the main road behind us, and the headlights of the passing cars. The ground was wet from a downpour earlier and we had to step lightly so we didn't spray our jeans with mud. It was a strange sensation to be there at night, without adults. I'd only ever been up there during the day, when Dad had to collect one of the neighbour's boys. I kept my head down on those occasions, staring at the dashboard so that none of the boys would see my face collapse into itself with embarrassment. Each time that had happened I had to lock myself in the bathroom when we got home and apply heavy eye make-up and line my lips and pout, wondering what to make of myself, and what boys would possibly make of me. The longer I looked the more uncertain I became. I'd get lost in the reflection of my own eyes. Then I'd get to thinking there was nothing behind them.

The front of the school loomed larger than it did during the day, and only the bare bulb above the porch at the main entrance gave off any light. All the windows were black. A priest stood silhouetted in the doorway, arms folded, legs akimbo, nodding to passers-by. I wanted to walk up to him and confess, have my sins absolved before I'd even committed them, before I was even sure what they might be. I wanted him to touch me, lay his lukewarm hands on my shoulders.

The older girls hanging round the front of the school looked unfazed by the smell of cheap eau de cologne. I spotted a few girls from our year arriving with boys from the town.

'Shall we have a cig, Mar?' I said.

'God, yeah,' Mar gasped. 'Not with *him* looking, though,' nodding towards the priest.

It was good that it was dark: it made it so much easier to walk past the other girls. And once around the corner we both had our backs flat against the cool dark-grey stone of the school wall, so that we could feel the dampness slowly trickle down our necks and cool our hot skin. Mar pulled a crumpled cigarette packet from the back pocket of her jeans: there were two flat cigarettes inside. She put hers straight to her lips and lit confidently, inhaling it like a deep-sea diver taking a final breath before plunging. Her eyes looked like fish eyes in the dim light. I rolled my cigarette slowly between middle finger and thumb, moulding it back into shape. Then I put it to my lips, lit it and inhaled deeply, holding it this time between index and middle finger, fearful that I might drop it or have to cough, and then relieved to find that I could exhale; and pleased by the aftertaste of ash on my tongue, and on the roof of my mouth, and the faint smell of lighter fuel under my nails. We held our cigarettes down by our sides, burning towards the dark wall, ready to be extinguished if any of the priests should happen to walk by.

More cars were arriving, more girls smelling of White Musk and coconut oil. The cold air tasted good after a cigarette. My limbs felt limp. The beers in the pockets of my jacket were stinging my hips. We walked to the edge of the bike shed, where the pale light from the porch stopped, and propped the cans by a tree stump. Everything went black as I rose from my hunkers. Mar's face came blurrily back into focus.

'We'll have those later, right Mar?'

She nodded. I knew if I'd said that we should just go home she'd have jumped at the chance, but there was no way we were going anywhere but in. Anyway, she'd nothing to be nervous about as far as I was concerned – she wasn't the one who was going to ask a strange boy to dance and then God knows what.

We followed the crowd, making our way to the back of the building – down dark blistered steps, wet from the rain earlier, leading into a puddled courtyard which ran the whole length of the school and was lit by the boys' classrooms along one side. At the end of this yard was a door into a fuzz of noise and dark. Just how I had imagined it. Mar put her arm in mine. We walked slowly. I was careful not to look directly into the bright classrooms in case I should catch the eye of some boy staring out at us. I didn't for a minute think that my boy would be gawping in that way, but I didn't want to look all the same.

ᘓ

The priest at the door looked blankly at the pair of us.

'That'll be two pounds each, ladies.'

I thought I noticed a glint of recognition in his eyes, which made me go puce as I fumbled in my too-tight jeans pocket for the money. I was sure he'd be on the phone to my parents.

'Come on now, we haven't got all day,' he said, his sneery head bobbing ever so slightly from side to side. Why was it all priests had black hair, I was wondering to myself. One of the coins fell through his fingers and he looked at me like I was an awful fool.

'Come on now, ladies, that's it, in you go.'

I looked back and he was busy assessing the length of the queue. Not interested in us at all.

The hall seemed empty as we stepped inside. Groups of boys and girls huddled against the walls on either side. The boys on stage were bashing out some REM cover – the lead singer, who was decked out in pyjamas, had the microphone in his mouth so you couldn't make out a word. The drummer looked like it was past his bedtime. As I got used to the dim light I could see that the older boys were loitering to the right of the stage; the younger ones fidgeted in the darker corners at the back of the hall; and girls of all ages filled the wall space between the two. The fumes from the aftershave were deadly.

A couple of young priests were selling soft drinks down the back, winking at their students affectionately and serving cans of soda to the girls with a reverential nod of the head, as if they were eternally grateful to us for offering a distraction to the boys for an evening. I noticed a couple of the neighbours who I used play with as a child but hadn't spoken to in years. Some of them looked like men now. One in particular, I remembered myself and my cousin being nasty to. He was smaller than us then, and very quiet, and we used to order him about for hours, then send him home whenever we got bored, shouting names at him. He nodded at me as we walked past, and I smiled and looked down at the ground.

We found a discreet place to stand, behind some older girls we didn't know. We didn't bother with the soft drinks just then, as we would have had to walk the entire length of the hall to get to the priests' makeshift stall. I couldn't help but notice boys looking in our direction. They were looking at Mar. She'd taken off her jumper and knotted it round her waist. It's funny how I hadn't really noticed before how beautiful she was: her dark shiny hair, her flawless skin, her breasts. How could boys keep their eyes off her? *I* couldn't, until she caught me staring at her and asked me if I was okay. It was so noisy she had to put her mouth right up to my ear.

'It's bloody loud, isn't it?'

'Sure is. Do you want to go outside and get those beers?'

'No, not yet. We only just got here.'

My ears were itchy inside with the vibrations of her voice. Then I noticed her whole body tauten, like the prairie dogs I'd seen in the zoo once on a school tour. Following her eyes I found a very pretty boy at the far side of the hall, about her height, maybe a little taller, with fine blond hair that flopped onto his bony face. He had vanilla-coloured skin. His shoulders were slightly hunched, and he had both hands firmly rooted in the pockets of his trousers. His eyes were glued to Mar.

'He's lovely,' I whispered, pulling her to me.

'Who? Oh, him? Yes, he is, isn't he. He's on my bus,' she said, her eyes flitting from mine to the other side of the room like she had bloody astigmatism. She was standing in such a way — back arched, hand on hip, head slightly tilted towards me — that allowed him a great view of the curve of her hips, her pert breasts, the wishbone curve of her chin, her flushed cheek. She couldn't stop herself grinning. I was done for then. She'd be off with him in no time, and I'd be left. There was no sign yet of my boy. He might not even show up. What would be worse? I couldn't be sure.

Her fella was at the older end of the hall. He must have been sixteen or seventeen. He was gawping right at her, and nudging his friends to do the same. And she didn't mind one bit. She chatted to me about this and that – stupid stuff I knew she didn't care about – pretending she hadn't noticed, or if she had she couldn't have cared less. She must have been used to boys staring at her: she went on that bus every day, after all, where all the boys would have copped a good eyeful.

It was getting very hot.

'How's it you didn't mention him before, Mar?'

She didn't answer me.

'You've perked up, haven't you?'

'What do you mean?' She gave me an evil look, then turned away again. 'Look. His friend's looking at you now, Lani. I'm sure he is,' she said, using her elbow to point.

I glanced over quickly and sulkily cast an eye over some boys jumping up and down to the music, near head-butting one another. Mar's boy wasn't moving. He was poised, much as she herself was, leaning slightly into the friend next to him – a lanky boy with dark hair and white skin. *My* boy. I caught the glare of his eyes (it looked like contempt), and quickly looked away. The room started to swim.

'Let's get those cans outside,' I said, my tongue going all big and hairy in my mouth.

'But he's cute. And he likes you. And anyway, I don't want to lose sight of them. Let's just go get a Coke or something, all right?'

I mutely agreed. We sidled our way through the crowd, which by that stage had grown considerably so that girls and boys were forced to mingle in the middle of the floor. The girls were hovering in little circles, showing off dance moves they'd practised for years in their bedrooms – like I'd done, watching my elephantine shadow gyrating on the ceiling and walls. The lads were getting more reckless, bumping into girls they fancied, pinching arses. It seemed like a bad idea once we'd started walking. Mar was right – we didn't want to lose sight of them. What if they thought we weren't interested? What if he met someone else in the time it took us to get from one end of that hall to the other?

'It's him,' I shouted.

'What?'

'It's *him*.'

She smirked. It irritated me, that smirk. It was deflating. She was too preoccupied with her bloody blossoming romance to care. It's funny, when I'd rehearsed this evening in my head it had never occurred to me that I'd be tetchy, or that Mar would have more important things to think about than the state of my bulging body. It did feel like it was bulging – like I was Alice in Wonderland and I was growing. I was going to break this school hall open with my huge limbs, and have all the girls and boys flee in terror or be crushed. Already I seemed to be at least a foot taller than everyone else there. They could all see me. I was a leaning tower that everyone could see from wherever they were in the hall. I was there at the corner of their vision. This must mean, then, that *he* could see me too. I stooped a little more. Even the priests we bought drinks from were smaller. One of them peered up at me. Christ, *she's* tall, he was probably thinking.

Mar was delighted with herself. 'Well, that's perfect.'

'What is?'

'That they're friends! It's fate. It must be!'

It wasn't so bad, sure, I reasoned with myself. At least he was there. And between us, me and Mar, we'd have those boys right where we wanted them – by standing at a safe distance, but within sight, ignoring them, and waiting. They'd know what to do next, and we'd know what to do once that happened. I swigged my Coke triumphantly as we made our way back to the exact spot we'd occupied before. It fizzed in my nostrils, making my eyes water.

There was no sign of them.

We waited. The band finished their set, and the disco music started. The hall was packed now, heaving with bodies. The walls were wet with condensation. Mar remained cool: she was sure they'd be back from wherever they'd gone. Still, I couldn't help feeling sick. I wanted to be in the cemetery, where I could watch him from a safe distance. Or at home, looking from behind the curtains in our front room.

One of the boys from the buses approached Mar. She talked easily with him, laughing, touching his arm, her face and neck reddening slightly as he walked away.

'He wants me to dance with him at the slow set. He

just sent that fella over to ask me. His name's Eoin. He's on my bus.'

'You told me that already.'

She didn't hear me. The excitement was too much. We both watched the boy walk over to Eoin, put his hand on his shoulder and pull him closer so he could talk directly into his ear. My boy appeared beside him, looking bored. I suppose that must have been how I looked.

Everyone stopped talking as the next song came to an end – all seemed to instinctively know that it was time. The hall fell silent and then, from out of this came the first chords of Bryan Adams' '(Everything I Do) I Do It For You'. No one dared move for a couple of seconds, then gradually a kind of slow-motion panic set in: a room full of evacuees with no exit, in danger of suffocating. Then the light-headedness from lack of oxygen as one, two, three couples made it to the middle of the dance floor without tripping or blushing. Mar pinched my arm as Eoin approached.

I was left alone before I even had time to catch her eye. I skulked further into the dark. My boy was still there. He didn't look like he was inclined to ask anyone anything. The music changed – still slow, but to something less *arresting*, I can't remember what now – and I felt myself being propelled across the room, towards him. 'I hope you don't mind – I've seen you up near my house – I was wondering – I'll understand if you – would you dance with me?'

He smiled, shrugged his shoulders and said he wouldn't mind. I was surprised to hear him speak. His voice sounded beautiful, I thought. He took my hand in his own and led me out to the floor. He was taller than me. He didn't smell artificial like the other boys. He smelled faintly of sweat, and greasy unwashed hair.

'Tell me your name.'

He pulled me to him so our groins were touching. I couldn't quite figure where to put my face so that we weren't breathing into one another, so I tilted it to the side, and glanced up at him, then away, quickly as I could.

'I'm Lani Devine,' I said. 'Who are you?'

'I'm Leon Brady. Haven't you heard of me?'

I shrugged. He squeezed his hands a little tighter around my waist. I should have been offended, but I couldn't be. All sorts of little fireworks were going off inside me, which made me even surer that I'd been right all along to fall in love with Leon Brady. I knew that if I looked long or hard enough at him he would kiss me, so I held my face to the side for another song. We didn't speak. Then he loosened his grip a little, I looked up at him, and his face moved towards mine. Our swaying stopped. The room went quiet, and he pulled me in, even tighter this time, and kissed me slowly on the mouth. I moved my hands from his hot back to the dark downy hair on his neck. Then the music speeded up again, and we were the only people standing still.

He'd no qualms about leading me directly outside after that. I had to breathe in short, shocking little breaths so he wouldn't hear me. The veins in my wrists and temples were pulsating so wildly I thought I might have a heart attack, and how embarrassing would that be, to die of a heart attack at the age of fifteen, just because a boy had danced with you and kissed you for a minute, and was taking you outside for a shift. The only other time I'd been kissed was by this bog-hopper wearing a Bon Jovi T-shirt when I was about twelve. He smelt faintly of sheep. My older cousin put me up to it. I didn't understand a word he said. I didn't even catch his name. And there was no one more surprised than me to find his cold slobbering tongue in my mouth. But this. This was exactly as I'd meant my first kiss to be. This became the official first kiss.

He didn't even make eye contact with the priest at the door, though I could see him looking at us disapprovingly. I wondered if he'd called my parents yet, though I knew it was stupid to think he would. Right then, anyway, I didn't really care what he or anyone else did.

It was cold out there, especially after the humidity of the hall. My clothes shrank icily onto my skin. Leon put his arm around my waist, which felt good, better than anything.

We were walking towards the playing fields then, at the back of the school, up the steps, past the bike shed, past the squash court — a dark concrete chasm where I could see the outlines of couples kissing, like shrimps in dark water — then along a path that cut between a football pitch and some tennis courts. The path was muddy, and there was a biting wind. It must have taken two or three minutes to get that far, and we hadn't said two words to each other.

I broke the silence.

'I've seen you before.'

'You said.'

'Yeah, up near my house.'

'I like to keep an eye on you.'

'Very funny.'

I was shivering. He took off his jumper and offered it to me. It was damp with sweat: I thanked him and wrapped it around my shoulders. We sat on a bench near the goalposts at the far end of the pitch.

'I go up there to see my mother,' he said. 'She's buried up there.'

The only person I'd ever known who died was Lazy Bones, and that was when I was nine or so. I don't remember feeling sad. All I remember was the purple and yellow bruise on his forehead, and the grown-ups in the room mumbling decades of the rosary, and a desperate desire to go outside and play with the neighbours' children. Lazy Bones's death reminded me of summer; of golden straw bales we climbed on in the fields behind my grandparents' house; and the wall we used to walk on, pretending we were tightrope artists.

'Oh God, I'm sorry,' I said.

I didn't know what else to say. People never do, they're not supposed to, are they.

'That's all right. She died when I was very young.'

'That's terrible,' I said, wanting desperately for us to change the subject, but not knowing how to without seeming rude or insensitive.

'She was from England. You ever been to England?'

'No, I haven't.'

'So how's it you asked me to dance?' he said then, all brazen.

'I don't know. Because I wanted to.'

And he pulled me to him again, pressed his mouth to mine, and kissed me long and dark. A dark kiss. One cold hand moved up under my T-shirt and slipped under my bra, pinching a nipple until it stung slightly. The other was grappling with the belt on my jeans, and my whole body tingled with fear and excitement. I pulled his hand from my belt, and he moved it down between my legs. I could feel the warmth of his palms on my thighs. I grabbed a clump of his hair, and we sank into each other. When we both came to he held my gaze and kind of mumbled we'd better head back, that the disco would be over soon, and that I was beautiful. Only my mother had ever told me I was beautiful. He wanted to see me again, but couldn't tell me when. That was the happiest I'd ever been, that I could remember.

We found Mar and Eoin waiting for us at the main entrance at the front of the school. They moved apart as they saw us approach, both of them folding their arms, and Eoin and Leon grinning at one another. Mar and I didn't know where to look. Her cheeks and lips were pinker and plumper than usual. I returned Leon's jumper and we snogged quickly, embarrassed in front of the others, and said our goodbyes. Mar and Eoin did the same, and then Mar was jaunting along beside me – up the steps, and down the driveway towards the main road and home.

'That was my first kiss, you know,' she said, all pleased with herself, as we stepped onto the road. She told me how she'd gone to the squash court with him, where she could hear the snorting of other couples shifting but couldn't see them in the dark. How Eoin had unzipped his trousers and pulled her hand down so she could feel his willy, hard as anything. How he made her move her hand up and down it. And how he pushed it against her.

'You didn't *do* it, did you?'

She laughed. 'What if we did?'

I didn't tell her about Leon pushing himself up against me, and putting his hand up under my T-shirt, and how much I'd liked it. I felt it must be wrong to like it so much.

We were quiet the rest of the way home, lost in our own thoughts.

Mam and Dad had forgotten to leave the light on in the front porch. We tippy-toed around the side. A broad band of light lay across our path as we turned the corner to the backyard. It was from my bedroom. Dad was standing directly under the bare light bulb, staring at my unmade bed. His face was pale, his expression pained and fixed. It was like I'd died or something. Mar grabbed my arm, startled, and her whole body froze. We stood in the shadows, just to the left of the window, watching, whispering.

'Jesus, Lani, what's going on?'

'I don't know. What the fuck are we going to do?'

I was horrified. This was something I didn't want Mar to see – my father distraught, confused.

Her face looked odd. It was like she had a bone stuck in her throat. Then I thought maybe something had happened to Gran. I jerked forward, out of the shadows, and Dad glanced out at me, squinted a little, and turned and left the room. It was like I was a ghost, my room a brightly lit tomb.

The two main lights were on in the living room, the lamps, the strip lights under the kitchen cupboards. Mam was stooped over the phone. I saw Dad touch her arm and signal that I was outside, and that I was coming in. I thought they might barricade the door, splash it with holy water. They both looked up as they heard the creaking of the handle, watched Blue scamper to my feet, panting excitedly. I brushed past her, Mar behind me.

'Where the hell have you been?' my father asked.

'Nowhere. At Mona's, like we said.'

I was trying to look directly at them, but I just couldn't. So I looked at the wall behind their heads instead.

Mam was near to tears.

'No you haven't. We phoned her mother to see if you wanted a lift home, and she said you weren't there. That you were never there. We've been frantic with worry.'

'But I *told* you they'd give me a lift home . . .'

'What are you *talking* about? You weren't *there*. Where the hell were you?'

There was no way of getting around this.

'We went to the disco.'

Dad's eyes went all bleary.

'Down the road. We were only down the road.'

'For Jesus' sake, why didn't you ask us if you could go? At least we would have known where you were. I was just about to call the guards.'

'We thought you'd been killed,' Mam croaked, and then she started to cry.

I didn't know what to say. I was the answer to their prayers, wasn't I? What did they think could have happened to me? It was such a small place, such a quiet place . . .

'Your mother's on her way over, Mar,' Mam said curtly. She could barely bring herself to look at her.

Mar was close to tears herself. 'Thanks, Mrs Devine,' was all she said. 'Sorry, Mrs Devine.'

Margaret, 15

My ma died when I was twelve. After, my sister found me trying to hang myself from a rafter in the cowshed. If that wouldn't have worked I would have tried the pond, though I didn't really fancy drowning in that muck.

They didn't know what to do with me. They thought the nuns would knock some sense into me, I suppose.

Ma'd been ill for a long time. I begged her not to leave me, but towards the end she didn't even know what I was saying to her. At least then I thought she'd have gone to heaven. I'm not even sure I believe in it anymore.

The first thing I remember when I got here is being given a pair of boots that were about two sizes too small. I had to walk around in them for months. Josie warned me not to ask for other ones or I'd get a right comeuppance.

It's funny, I was so scared I couldn't even kill myself. I'd rather have stayed alive than run into that Mother Andrew at night, with her cane strapped to her waist and her beady eyes boring holes in me. I'd end up having to get up at night anyway, because I'd wet the bed I was so scared. Then I'd have to sneak down to the laundry to wash the sheets and sneak back again and put them on the bed sopping. If I got caught I was whipped across the backside with a birch. One time I got hit with a bit of an orange box that had nails in it. I still have scars on my arm.

I was lucky because I was good at school, so they didn't take me out to work in the convent. I prefer being at school.

I'm getting out of here next year. My father says he will come and get me. I don't want to kill myself anymore. I'm going to go away to England and learn to be a nurse, so I can make people better, so other children aren't left on their own like me.

⌘

Thanks, Mrs Devine. Sorry, Mrs Devine. Why couldn't Mar have opened her fat gob instead of just standing there. She could have tried to explain . . . When her mother came to pick her up she gave her that look, like she just wanted to be taken home and tucked up in bed. Like butter wouldn't melt in her mouth. Like I'd put her up to it.

She was there at the gate on Monday morning. I walked straight past her.

'You can eff right off,' I said, as she tugged on the strap of my bag.

'But Lani, I need to talk to you about something.'

'Yeah, well, I don't need to talk to *you*. Ever.'

That told her.

School was unbearably dull. I didn't want to have to think about anything else but Leon Brady. And not being able to talk about him with anybody was so frustrating. I felt like I would burst.

The only tolerable classes were English and 'free'. English was up in my favourite classroom on the second floor of the old building, overlooking the playing fields and the temporary lake from the flooding, which changed from pewter to a murky green to black in places. There were two swans on it, and it was quite pleasant to watch them while listening to Mr Breslin read from *The Winter's Tale*.

I was made to stand in a musty corner of the concert hall at 'free', for passing notes. I liked it there.

By mid-afternoon maths I was worn out – stifled by the billowing hot dusty air from the radiators, the constant droning of the teachers' voices and the insufferable feeling that I had somehow made a fool of myself, or Leon had made a fool of me and would never want to set eyes on me again. I hadn't even let him touch me *down there*, and Mar had probably gone all the way, knowing her.

I was frigid.

And I hadn't said anything funny or smart.

And I wasn't pretty like Mar.

Mam and Dad didn't stay cross for long. All was forgiven by the end of the week. Forgotten, anyway. Mam was too preoccupied with the pregnancy. And once Dad was over the trauma of thinking I was dead he was back to his usual self – out in the garden mostly, or in the shed, knocking together some shelves to go around the fireplace in the front room.

Mam had taken to sewing again, which she hadn't done since I was small.

'I used make all your clothes,' she told me more than once. I remembered well. Even my First Holy Communion dress she made — mostly because I was too big to fit into any of the bought ones. We even made a trip across the border to try and find one, but the best we came across there was an off-white two-piece Confirmation suit. Frilly skirt and blouse with pearl buttons. I wanted one of those meringue ones like the normal-size girls in my class.

'There wasn't a thing I couldn't make. And now look at me. I can barely sew on a button.'

But she soon got the hang of it, hammering away at the stiff old treadle of our Singer sewing machine. A cot-size duvet cover first, with zoo animals peeking from behind coloured squares. Then a large raggedy doll, about four feet tall. She spent hours stuffing that doll with old tights, hand-sewing her torso together, adding arms, legs, a head; drawing on and embroidering a face that had just the right blandness of expression so as not to frighten the poor baby. There was the wool hair, and the clothes. Even little socks and shoes.

Friday afternoon art class, Mrs Smith announced we'd be going to the boys' school the following week, to hear a local artist talk about her work. The thought of going back there filled me with a kind of joy I can't rightly explain. Chances were I wouldn't even see Leon, but just to be in the same building as him would be enough. It didn't even bother me that other boys would be there.

CR

There I was in the library, a bright, high-vaulted white room. I'd never been in the likes of it. The library in our school was functional, beige, with chipboard shelving and orange plastic desks; with tatty old paperback copies of romance novels. The library in town wasn't much better. *This* library was something else. All the volumes on the shelves were beautifully leather-bound. Whole sets of blue, dark brown, maroon volumes – of Dickens, Thackeray, Austen – sat on the mahogany shelves that stretched right up to the corniced ceiling. The windows, too, were from ceiling to floor, halved by orange blinds. There were dust motes swimming in the sunlight.

We were seated at the front of the room, the boys filed in behind us. Mrs Smith hovered around us protectively. If we turned round, God forbid, we'd be turned to salt or stone.

I really wished Mar was beside me then. I was missing her terribly. I had to make do with Mona instead – the famous Mona we famously didn't go visiting that night – who, as her name implied, enjoyed a good old whinge. It wouldn't have surprised me if she'd gotten the hump while everyone else waited piously for the boys to be seated. She didn't, though, she kept her mouth shut.

The boys were much louder than us. Chair legs screeched across the wooden floor, knocked against one another, the rubber soles of shoes squeaked. They muttered among themselves as we wouldn't dare. Their teachers were drawing them in in hushed tones, as if into a pen. I imagined they had sticks and were lightly whipping their flanks, as farmers did with their herds, grunting orders that weren't words. Then I could feel their grunting at my neck, as they leaned forward to sit down. Mona glanced around contemptuously as one boy kneed her in the back. He didn't apologise. We were on their turf. And we were girls. Fifteen-year-old boys were only barely human, as far as I was concerned.

The artist was introduced and off she went, talking about her house out in the woods, near one of the lakes, and how the water inspired her work. And what a watery place we lived in, even though it was inland. And she liked to work in blue. And she sounded kind of blue – not blue *sad* but blue *cold*. I drifted off. I wanted to be alone in the library. Or hiding somewhere, like I could do at home, watching Leon earnestly searching through the books for a favourite poem he wanted to learn by heart. I wanted to drop a bowl of marbles on the wooden floorboards, for the sound it would make.

The thought that Leon was there, in the same building, that he had been in this same room many times before – maybe even that day – filled me with the sort of happiness I'd felt when I was small, playing make-believe – that under this tree is my house, in this stone bowl of mud and elderberries a magic potion, in that hollow in the field a glistening pool, and all is blissful and exactly how I want it to be, and have made it be. I conjured up the kiss. And it was like there were tiny droplets of water trickling over my skin.

Just then I felt a gentle prod in my back. I didn't move. If some boy was trying to wind me up, get me into trouble, it wasn't going to work. He prodded again – harder this time – between my ribs. I tried desperately to concentrate on what the woman was saying. Then there was a faint swishing noise below my chair and something against my foot. I looked down: there was a white envelope with what looked like 'Lane' or 'Toni' scrawled on it.

CR

It was 'Lani' all right. Definitely 'Lani'. I leaned down, lifted
the envelope, and slipped it under the sleeve of my jumper.
It was small and slim. I didn't dare turn round to see who
it was had given it to me.

I couldn't wait to get home that afternoon. Our lift was late
as usual: it was our neighbour, Karen's father, who picked me
up Mondays and Wednesdays, when Mam was working in
Martin the vet's in town. We were sat for ages on the wall in
front of the Virgin Mary, kicking the gravel with the toes of
our shoes and talking about exams, teachers, anything to do
with school. We had little to say to each other besides. Not
since we'd fallen out when we were five or six had we had a
proper conversation. She'd hit me with a plastic spade, bang
on the forehead, in the sandpit in her back garden. I can't
remember what for, now: I don't think she liked me too much.
Or maybe I'd stolen her bucket. I went home crying to my
mother anyway. I had a big purple bruise over my right eye.

77

I desperately wanted to open the letter but knew that I couldn't with her beady little eyes stuck to me. She'd be telling her friends the next day: 'You should have seen the state of her. Red as a beetroot. Her hands shaking like leaves . . .' When I did finally get home I went straight to my room, shut the door and tore the envelope open. It was written on ruled A4 paper, the kind we used for science:

My darling Lani,

I dreamt last night that I was alone in a dark house. I walked upstairs to my room and you were lying there, naked, on my bed. I wanted desperately to touch you but couldn't reach you, couldn't walk through the doorway. You were like Ophelia, pale and beautiful.

I can't stop thinking about you. There were moments, the other night, when I felt so warm and comfortable with you, though it was cold out there. If I don't see you soon I think I might lose my mind. I know it is only days since we met, and that we barely know each other, have barely spoken, but it feels right. I'm not used to feeling this way.

L.B.

p.t.o. →

Farewell to last night!
The memory will not fade.
Though I were to die for it,
I wish that it were beginning now.

If you wish to respond to this please give letter to Geraldine McGovern (4th year), and it will reach me safely.

I couldn't believe it. I was afraid to believe it at first. It had to be some kind of joke. I could just see him sitting there in his dorm with some of the other boys, sniggering to themselves while they composed it. All of them thinking about touching me. Telling him what to write next. And to add that poem. I tried to dismiss it, but I couldn't. I wanted it to be true more than anything. A whole rake of emotions followed. Finally, after I'd cried, danced round the room, paced around the house a couple of times, I quietened down, got a pen and paper and sat down to draft a reply.

It wasn't easy. The idea of meeting him scared the life out of me. I wouldn't know what to say to him. And I didn't know where we could meet. I didn't want to suggest the cemetery, that would be weird, and I *was* going to write that I'd been grounded, but then I didn't want him knowing that I'd had to sneak out that night and that I was some kind of child. I wanted to include some lines from a poem, as he had done. I found Kavanagh's 'There will be bluebells growing under the big trees / And you will be there and I will be there in May' in an old book of poems on the shelf outside my room. I liked that line 'We will be interested in the grass', but then I realised it might have been the graveyard I was referring to, with the bluebells under the trees up there.

I was going to say I'd dreamt of him, but if I had I

couldn't remember. I'd dreamt of a baby – a little plasticine baby the size of my palm that I had to look after. I kept losing it behind the couch, or it would melt and fall off my hand. And I dreamt about being late for an exam that was being held in the church in town; and of running but not moving.

It took me hours to write that letter. I just couldn't find the words. Finally, I wrote:

Dearest Leon,

I was both surprised and delighted to hear from you. I feel the same way: if I do not see you soon I shall go insane. I shall walk into your dreams every night until I see you again.
Tell me when and where and I will be there.

  Love,
  Lani

Next day I walked up to Mar. She was crouched at the side of the shed on the laneway down from school with some bitch I couldn't stand. Sylvia, I think her name was.

'I need you to give this to Geraldine McGovern.' I held out the envelope.

'I thought you weren't talking to me,' she said, flicking ash from her cigarette onto her shoe.

'I'm not.'

'So why should I?'

'Because I'm asking.'

'*Hnph*.'

'All right then, don't bother,' I said, turning and walking away.

'All right, all right,' she called after me, 'give us it.'

I was afraid of what she'd do with it. She and Sylvia might just tear it open and have a right laugh at my expense. But I hadn't much choice.

She stuffed it into the top of her skirt, and the pair of them gave me the dirtiest look and burst out laughing.

'Sicko,' I heard one of them whisper, whatever that was supposed to mean.

CR

Dad picked me up at lunchtime on his way into town to collect Mam from work. I'd said I'd go with them for the first ultrasound. I suppose they thought I needed to see it with my own eyes to believe it. Anyway, I was glad to get away from school.

Mam had on one of her best outfits: a lemon and pink floral pleated skirt and V-neck short-sleeved blouse, with a pink cardigan draped over her shoulders. It was one of her summer outfits. The skirt had an elasticated waist — that would have been why she was wearing it in the middle of winter. She hadn't bought any maternity gear at that stage — too early — so she was probably running out of clothes that fitted right. She looked kind of other-worldly in her unseasonal outfit.

'Are you not cold?' I said to her.

'No, I'm grand,' she said, pulling the cardigan tighter around her shoulders. I could see the goosebumps on her arms.

Dad couldn't hide his excitement. 'Boy or girl, what do you think, eh girls?'

I sighed and looked out the window.

'We won't be able to tell at this stage, love.'

'Well, my money's on a boy. What do you think, Lani?'

Shut your fat mouth, is what I *wanted* to say.

'Don't know. I'd say a girl.'

'Why do you say that, Lani?' Mam turned to me on the back seat, surprised I'd said anything at all.

'Just.'

Just because I felt like it. Just as something to say to shut him up.

'*Just*,' he laughed.

Mam brushed some stray hairs from Dad's shoulder, leaving her elbow to rest on the back of his seat. From where I was sitting you'd have thought the two of them were off to Bundoran for the day.

The last time I'd been to the hospital was to visit Gran after she'd had her stroke. I thought that was goodbye then. They were sunny days just like this one. She kept asking me to take her home – 'Take me home, Lani. Please love, take me home' – and I'd look at Mam and she'd shrug her shoulders.

'You'll be going home soon, Mammy,' she'd say, loudly and slowly so that Gran could decipher the words.

Gran'd say other things too that I couldn't make out at all. It was like someone had stuffed her mouth with cotton wool. And those words I could make out were coming out all wrong.

She couldn't go home again – not on her own.

Uncle Patrick was over from England that time. Gran's face would light up when she saw him. Her only son, a priest. He didn't stick around for long though. He worked in a shelter in London and only had a few days' leave, he said, he'd be needed back there. He'd come to say goodbye too, though he tried not to let on. He stayed in Gran's empty house, which struck me as a very odd thing to do. When I asked Mam why he wouldn't come stay with us she just said he wanted to spend some time in his own room, that he needed time to reflect, and that our house was strange to him. His room in the home-place was kept just as he'd left it – the same pictures on the walls, the football trophies, even the bedclothes. The wallpaper was coming away in places, and the sheets always felt damp whenever I'd stayed over. Patrick didn't come anywhere near our house the few days he was home.

Gran kept asking for Celia, that time she was ill. It was the first time I'd heard her say her name. I'd seen the photo on the mantelpiece, of course, and Mam had told me she was her half-sister, but I didn't really understand until then.

Mam wouldn't know what to say. She'd get especially uncomfortable if Uncle Patrick was there. He'd get all fidgety and make some excuse to leave the room. 'I'll go get us some tea, will I?' he'd say. He had black hair too. He didn't look at all like Mam. He was the spit of Lazy Bones, apparently, his father's son.

Gran wouldn't let on who Celia's father was then. I'm

surprised, now that I think of it, that Mam let me listen to all this. I suppose she thought I was so young I wouldn't understand. She wanted Celia, Gran kept saying, where was Celia. My mother promised her she'd find her, and then nothing more was said of it. I used to wonder if I'd dreamt the whole thing, it was so muddled in my head.

'Those are the maternity wards, Lani.'

Mam pointed to the bay windows at the front that opened out onto a patio, and then down to a manicured lawn with leafless cherry blossoms.

'That's where you spent your first few days.'

'The last time I was here was to see Gran,' I said.

'Oh, so it was. We thought she'd not be leaving that time, didn't we, Dad?'

I hated the way they called each other 'Mam' and 'Dad' for my benefit, as if I was still a child. I was sure they didn't call each other that in private – when their condom broke, for example: 'Oh no, Dad, what are we going to do?'

The nurse was late. We sat on a bench in the corridor, the blood-red leather creaking beneath us. Hospital staff walked quickly past in their crisp antiseptic garments. A pretty doctor smiled at me as she went by, chart in hand. I wanted to be like her, with her pale blonde hair and her white coat. A porter and a nurse pushed an old man past on a trolley. He was all entangled, strings tied loosely around his green paper dress, a drip in his arm, a tube curling from his mouth. They were quiet and slow: no emergency, they must have been heading for theatre.

Mam was taken into the prenatal room first, where she could remove her blouse and pull her elasticated skirt down round her hips. She was given a paper dress like the man on the trolley.

'And how have you been feeling, Deirdre?' the nurse was asking when Dad and I walked in.

'Oh, quite sick still. And tired. And *hungry all the time!*'

They both laughed.

'Well, hopefully the nausea will pass soon – in a week or two. Try eating lots of small meals rather than three big ones. Dry biscuits or toast can help.'

'Yes, I've been doing that,' Mam said peevishly, and quickly tried to make amends for her rudeness by offering, 'My breasts have been *particularly* sensitive this week.'

I could feel the muscles on my face slacken with embarrassment. Dad cleared his throat. All that discomfort bubbling out of him, breaking on the surface.

'Oh, yes, I know. That can be a terrible problem. There isn't really much we can do about that I'm afraid, my dear. I would just recommend that you wear good strong sports bras. And you could try rubbing some nice cold cream into them? It's not a cure but it feels lovely!'

'I'll do that then,' said Mam cheerily.

Dad and I didn't know where to look.

'Right so,' said the nurse, as she lifted back the paper from my mother's belly, 'let's have a look.'

Mam's belly was ever so slightly distended, as though someone had taken a foot pump to it – the same taut and shiny complexion as an inflated beach ball or one of our inflatable camp beds. A faint line running from her belly button down to her knicker-line (which I imagined leading to the nozzle for the pump). The nurse smeared what looked like a computer mouse with a clear gel and placed it on Mam's tummy. She swept it over and back, then stopped, her eyes all the time on the screen to the right of Mam's head.

'Ooh, that's cold.'

'I'm sorry, dear.'

'Oh, not at all.'

Our eyes went from the movement of the nurse's hand, to the screen, to her hand, to the screen, waiting for something to pop into focus.

'There you go, you see?' she said, sounding slightly relieved. 'There's the head, and this' – with her finger she followed a tiny curve on the screen – 'this is the spinal cord. See how tiny it is? A perfectly healthy little foetus.'

We all squinted. If you squinted really hard, a vague little creature, like a dormouse, blurred into focus. Dad squeezed Mam's hand, kissed the top of her head. A great sigh of something, I wasn't really sure what it was, heaved from my body. Mam grabbed my hand, pulled me to her, and we all stayed there like that for what seemed like an age – Dad with one hand on my back, my head on Mam's shoulder and one arm dangling by my side. Mam was crying. Dad might have been crying too, I couldn't see.

Mar came into class a couple of mornings later fluttering an envelope about, holding it out to me, then pulling it away.

'Just give it to me, would you?'

'Is that a *love* letter?' Mary Hart asked, grinning and elbowing her friend to look at me.

I said nothing.

'Hardly,' her friend scoffed.

'Just give it to me, Mar. You're not funny.'

I pulled at her jumper, and snatched it out of her outstretched hand.

'No need to have a fucking *hernia*, Lani.'

I slipped it between the pages of my English book in my school bag.

'You're such a fucking cow,' I said.

'That's the thanks I get,' she snorted, looking over at the other girls and throwing her eyes up to heaven. 'If I was you I wouldn't have anything to do with him,' she said.

'Well, I'm not you,' I said, 'thank God. And what would you know anyway?'

'That you're well away from him, is what.'

I read the letter over a ham sandwich at lunchtime.

Dear Lani,

My recurring dream of you, in my room, has changed. Last night I dreamed I was lying in my bed, and you came to me. You came right into my room, leaned over the bed, and kissed me. The gentlest kiss. How can I describe to you how happy that made me?

I can think of nothing else but you.

My study has gone by the wayside these past few days, but I don't care. I cannot wait to see you again — to see those blue eyes of yours, your golden hair. Can you come out to Crogher on Saturday? To Bannon's pub on the square at 2 o'clock. I'll wait for you. I'll know, if you're not there, that you have thought better of all of this, and I'll understand (but I do so hope you turn up!). I'll pray every night (though I don't believe in God) for you to come, my darling Lani.

> *We will not die, these lovers say,*
> *For any eyes but eyes of blue;*
> *No hair shall win our hearts away*
> *But hair of golden hue.*

Love,
L.B.

I tore the middle section from a copybook and quickly wrote:

Dear Leon,

I will do my very best to be there on Saturday. I'll get my bike out. I haven't used it in a long time, so I'm afraid I might be a bit red in the face when you see me!

I've never been to Bannon's but I think I know the one you mean. I'll see you there at 2. I hope you get this letter before then. If not I suppose it doesn't really matter, either way.

Love,

Lani

I had to go up to Geraldine McGovern in the canteen and ask her if she'd give the letter to Leon so I wouldn't have to talk to Mar. I nearly died of embarrassment. She looked at me like I was a piece of dog shit.

CR

I hadn't ever been in a pub on my own. I'd thought it would be empty on a Saturday afternoon. Once my eyes got used to the dark inside, though, and my nostrils to the smell of turf and tobacco smoke, I saw the string of locals all propped up at the bar. It looked like a family reunion – small children, grandparents and all. They weren't too happy to see me. Not one of them said hello. There was no one behind the bar, and there was no sign of Leon, so I turned and walked straight out again.

I was just about to mount my bike so I could pretend to be leaving and circle the town for a bit, hoping Leon would show up, when the youngest of the family group came out and prodded me in the leg with his finger. He couldn't have been more than four or five.

'What the fuck are you doing here?' he asked.

I laughed. I couldn't help it.

'Who the fuck do you think you are?'

He was very cute. But I was also a little intimidated. So I stopped laughing, in case one of his older brothers decided to come and sort me out. He started kicking me then, on the shins, and shouting, 'Who the fuck . . . who the fuck do you think you are?'

'And who are you?' I asked quietly, wincing a bit as he kicked me again really hard.

He stopped then, looked up and said: 'None of your fuckin' business.'

I heard laughter behind me. Here we go, I thought, the older brother. But it was Leon. He smiled at me (the first time I ever saw him smile), and told the little brat to get lost, which he did.

'Aren't you a little scared of him?' I asked, mortified.

'And why would I be scared of that little shite?'

He took my hand and we headed for the road that led to the forest park.

'Are we going to your house?'

'Maybe later,' he said, pulling me in the direction of the woods. 'I live up that way,' he pointed, 'out towards the football grounds. See that there,' he said, pointing now at a tiny white cottage with a thatched roof, 'that's that artist's house, the one you saw in school the other day.'

'And how did you know I'd be there? I got an awful fright when I felt that lad prodding me in the back.'

'Don't I know everything there is to know about you.'

'Do you now?'

'Of course.' He grabbed my wrist, held it tightly. 'I like

that top you have on you,' he said, glancing down at it. 'Is it new?'

I blushed. 'No. Why?'

'Oh, I don't know.'

It was fairly low-cut, and though I was mortified, I was pleased too that he'd noticed.

'You're good at writing,' I said, trying to draw attention away from my breasts then, as I could feel my face and neck redden. It only made it worse, though. I felt like I was talking too quickly, slurring my words. 'Do you read lots?'

'I don't like to read. Have to read enough at school as it is.'

'But what about that poem?'

'Oh, I thought it would impress you. Girls like that kind of stuff, don't they.'

We walked along in silence for a few moments. I looked up at him and saw that he was grinning to himself.

'Ha ha, very funny,' I said.

I wanted the ground to open up and swallow me.

The road turned into a laneway that grew darker under the shadow of the blue spruce. The lake was just visible over the hill. I'd been out there many times with Mam and Dad. We spent whole days there in summer, swimming, picking big bunches of wild flowers, making daisy chains, following the arrows through the woods past the little Hansel-and-Gretel style keeper's lodge, with its boarded-up windows. I'd go around holding buttercups under the grown-ups' chins to see who liked butter. It seemed they all did, but I still had to make sure with each new buttercup I picked. The fields around the lake were full of those pale violet cuckoo flowers, and cuckoo spit.

It was out there that I first learned to swim. I can't remember that very moment when I was able to float, but I remember the fear of the deep and the large pike I saw Dad and the other fishermen haul from the water, and the slimy feel of the bed of the lake. Blue loved the water. She went in after the flies. We had big picnics in the long grass, away from the lake and the midges, and I'd lie flat looking up at the sky.

It was cold now. And it was much quieter.

We made our way down to the water and crossed the bridge. I liked the sound our feet made on the wood. I always liked that sound. There wasn't a soul around. The big oaks at the other side of the bridge were bare of leaves, and the ground was covered in a brown pulp of pine needles, bark and dead leaves. A squirrel scuttered up one of the trees in front of us, and we both stopped to look, then moved on, round by the edge of the lake, on a footpath that was well worn by fishermen and bathers. I wanted to put my toes in the water, though it was cold and the water would be even colder. Our clenched hands were damp, but I didn't want to let go of him. He moved closer to me. I could feel his breath on my neck. He smelled warm and greasy, as before. I felt a hotness down my back, though the rest of me was shivering. I buried my free hand in the pocket of my coat.

'Are you sure my bike will be okay back there?' I asked, trying to distract myself from the thought of lying down on the wet grass with him.

'It'll be fine,' he said, 'don't worry,' and he held my gaze for a long enough time that we were forced to move closer together and kiss. His tongue was cold. His hands moved up under my coat, my jumper, my top, and I felt their watery print on my clammy back. The lake made a nice lapping sound. I pushed against him, as hard as I could. His breathing was coarse and uneven, like mine. I dug my hands into his thick hair, as if I was trying to unearth something, and his hands moved across my flesh – up and down my back, around to my belly and my breasts. He took hold of my throat, pushed his tongue further into my mouth until I thought I would drown and had to pull back.

I wanted him to do what he would with me, but I didn't have the words to tell him, so I took his hand again and led him away from the water and into a part of the woods where no one would see us if they happened past.

The ground was a dark mulch away from the footpath. We found an opening in the wood where it was still damp and spongy, but less sodden. Leon threw his coat down over some wet bracken and pressed it to the ground. Damp patches seeped up through it. I sat down first. He looked uncomfortable then for the first time. I patted the bit of coat beside me to encourage him, and he sat down. He put an arm around my waist and looked straight ahead of him. His little finger hooked itself in the top of my jeans. I was admiring his pouting mouth and the dark growth of stubble just under his lower lip, waiting for him to make the next move. He pulled tufts of moss from the tree beside him. A woodlouse ran over his finger and he pulled his hand away quickly and shivered.

'Let's get out of here.'

The wet was through to my skin.

'Look, you're drenched,' he said.

'Oh, I don't mind, really.'

'No, let's just go.'

'Can't we go back to yours, then?'

'No, my dad's there—'

We followed the path round, past the bathing area, then away from the water, into the woods again. The cracking of broken branches underfoot, and the birds. I didn't know where he was leading me. I'd never come this way before: I always thought it was a dead end there, just beyond the changing area.

'Where are we going?'

I wasn't sure what I'd done wrong. He was biting the top of a biro he'd pulled from inside his coat pocket.

'If you're not careful with that pen, you'll end up with blue lips.'

It was like he hadn't heard me.

'I have to go and put the spuds on for Dad's dinner,' he said, which made no sense.

Back to the main road again – a full circle of about a half mile – without uttering another word. He still had my hand in his, and he squeezed it every now and again, very gently.

I was relieved to see my bike hadn't been touched, and that that little boy wasn't around.

'I'm sorry,' he said.

'What are you sorry for?'

'For not taking you to my house. I just can't. Maybe some other time.'

'It doesn't matter,' I said, though really it did matter. I wanted so desperately for him to keep me there, not send me away. And I wanted to see where he lived. I don't know why, I just did. And all that fresh air had made me hungry, and I had to cycle all the way home now on an empty stomach. We kissed goodbye. I heard his stomach grumble.

'Thanks for coming out.'

'It was lovely.'

I didn't think I'd see him again after that. Tears poured down my face as I cycled home. I was so hungry by the time I got there, but I had to hide it. I couldn't have Mam and Dad thinking I'd been in town all that time and not bothered to get a bite to eat.

Angela, 17

I'm going to work in one of them big stores in Dublin, Switzers or Clerys. Mother Assumpta says I have a real gift with my hands. I'm going to be a respectable woman. Some nice young fella will marry me – I'll make the dress myself – and we'll have four children: Patricia, Martin, Gemma and Michael. Girl, boy, girl, boy. They'll all have blonde curls. They'll none of them be redheads like me. I do sometimes help Mother Michael with the babies down in the infirmary, to practise for when I have my own.

Mother Assumpta tried to pretend once like she was my husband! Sitting me on her lap and her saying things like 'Where's the dinner, woman?' which made me laugh. And her rubbing her hands up me the way men are supposed to. And then didn't Mother Carmel walk in!

I have special privileges since. Mother Carmel says

I've earned them. I sit at a separate table in the refectory, away from the young ones. I get tea and toast every morning in the convent kitchen. And I don't get beat anymore.

Mother Felix says I'm awful hard-working. Me and Mary make all of the clothes for the girls. Blue serge dresses and pinafores for the winter, and white calico dresses for the summer. But that's not why I get special privileges. It's because I can do embroidery. I make table mats and underwear, and then they sell them outside. Someday I'd like to make a big tablecloth, but that would take an awful long time.

My mother comes to see me sometimes. The last time she was here she told me that a friend of hers had been to Lourdes with her aunt, who is in a wheelchair. She swore she'd seen my table mats on sale on one of them stalls there, only she couldn't stop to take a closer look because she was in one of them processions of the Virgin Mary. We were both almost in tears, thinking of my table mats beyond there in Lourdes.

I've been here since I was nine. We were living at my grandparents'. I don't know where my father was. I never dared ask. Then my grandmother died and my mother had to spend all her time looking after my grandfather. She couldn't do that and look after us too. She tried for a while but she couldn't cope. Me and my brothers were better off being sent to get a proper education. I didn't mind at first because it was easier than doing the work on the farm. I had big abscesses on my hands from that. But then the chilblains were just as bad. I thought I'd die of cold. My feet would hurt so much I'd chew the inside of my mouth off. And I couldn't stand Mother Carmel beating the little ones. I didn't mind if it was me, I was used to it. But I couldn't stand the little ones being beaten. Someday God will give her a good beating before he lets her set foot inside the gates of heaven.

One of my brothers came to see me when he was grown up and left the school he was sent to. I didn't even recognise him. He's working in Dublin now. He says I'd love Clerys. He says it's jam full of hats and handbags and silk scarves. He says I'd make a fine seamstress. I've never heard anyone called that before. I told Mary and she thinks I'm daft.

My brother gave me a picture of himself and Michael, the other one. You can hardly tell them apart. I showed it to Mary and she blushed bright pink. Maybe she'll marry one of them and we'll be sisters-in-law! The gardener's son winks at me every morning when I walk past him from the refectory to the convent. He does it to make me go red. I try not to look at him but if I don't he'll only start whistling at me like I'm a dog and calling me 'Rua', and then I go even more red.

❦

It was poker night at home that night. Gran was first to speak.

'Eighty pence,' she says.

'I'll see you,' Mam says, and throws in her eighty, a hint of a smile on her lips. Dad had folded already. Mary Reilly was undecided still. She hesitated, then:

'Feck it, I'll see you, and raise you,' she said, throwing £1.60 into the pot.

Everyone looked at Paddy to see what he would do.

'Ah, Jesus. You're an awful woman, Mary,' says Paddy.

Their concentration was waning, Mam's especially. She was the only sober one in the room. The rest of them were all looking a little red in the face with booze. Mary's eyes were out on sticks.

'Don't you know what I'm like, Paddy?'

'Only too well,' he moaned.

Dad leaned back in his chair, hands folded over his chest, with a look of the cat that got the cream.

'Right, that's it: I'm folding. Feck you, Mary,' Paddy said, and everyone laughed except Gran. The expression on her face hadn't changed from the start of the game.

'I'll raise it again,' she said, sliding the coins into the middle of the table, very carefully, with her good hand.

'Ah Christ, Mammy,' Mam said, 'that's me out too.'

Mary was too drunk to care. Her head swayed from side to side.

'Okay, okay, I'm out too. Show us what you have, Phil.'

Gran let her guard down and smiled her lopsided smile as she turned over her cards one by one, to reveal two low pairs.

'For Jesus' sake. I don't know how you do it, Phil. Fuck me!' Paddy shouted, and they all laughed.

'Paddy,' Mary scolded.

Dad topped up everyone's glasses. I'd filled big white hunks of bread with ham and coleslaw, and cheese and pickle, and placed them in a basket in the middle of the table along with a plate of sliced, buttered tea-brack Mam had made earlier.

'Ah sure, you're a great girl, Lani. And what would your Mam do without you,' Mary said.

She still talked to me like I was ten years old.

'That's a fine bit of cake, Deirdre,' Paddy said to Mam. 'Did you make that yourself?'

'I did. And speaking of cake, I have a bun in the oven,' she said, biting the nail on her index finger.

I wasn't sure I'd heard her right. I don't think anyone was. Even Dad looked a little taken aback.

'Yes, I'm pregnant.'

'Jesus, Mary and Joseph,' Mary screeched. 'Go 'way! That's fantastic news, Deirdre. When's it due?'

'May,' said Mam.

'Well, by God, Deirdre and Noel, you're a fine pair,' Paddy said as he stood up to walk around the table and hug the two of them, one after the other.

'It was an accident, of course,' Dad said, winking at him.

'Ah, you're an awful man, Noel Devine,' Paddy said, slapping him on the back.

'You're the first we've told. We wanted to wait until the three months were up, you know?' said Mam.

'Oh, of course, Deirdre. Of course,' Mary said, leaning over and putting her arm around her shoulder.

'And what about you, Lani? Are you delighted to be having a little brother or sister?'

'I am,' I said, 'I am,' and both Mam and Dad turned and looked at me. I was surprised at myself.

The phone rang. I ran out of the room to get it, glad to escape the limelight.

It was Leon.

'I got your number in the phone book.'

'Oh. I should have given it to you. I didn't expect to hear from you again though.'

'Why not?'

'I thought you were annoyed at me.'

'What would I be annoyed at you for?'

'I don't know.'

'I can't stay on long,' he said.

I could hear a television on loud in the background, and a man's voice whinging at Leon to get off the phone.

'I was wondering if you'd like to meet tomorrow evening, maybe? I could come out to the house. It's that last one on the left just before the cemetery, isn't it?' He was almost whispering.

Of course I knew I couldn't have him anywhere near the house – Mam and Dad would have a fit – but I couldn't tell *him* that.

'That's right. Yes, that would be nice.'

'Okay, I'll see you tomorrow then. Around six?'

I must have looked a little flustered when I walked back into the living room. They all looked at me, sandwiches poised, waiting to hear who it was had been calling at that time of night. Paddy and Mary looked a little uneasy. They knew about that night and the guards nearly being called out. They knew everything that went on in our house.

'Who was that, calling at this hour?' Mam asked.

'Oh, just Mar.'

'The terrible twin,' Dad joked, and attention again focused on the sandwiches. The baby talk resumed.

'I had piles, you know, Deirdre. Had to sit on a rubber ring for *weeks*.'

'Jesus, Mary, I don't want to know,' my mother cringed.

They stayed up later than usual that night, celebrating. I heard Paddy and Mary leave just after two, and still I couldn't sleep.

❦

The doorbell rang at ten to six the next evening.

'Who's that, love? Who is it?' Gran was asking.

'Oh, I think it's just someone collecting for the parish,' I said, making sure to close the living room door behind me so's she wouldn't see. 'I've got it,' I shouted as loud as I could, so neither Mam nor Dad would be roused from whatever it was they were doing.

'Remember me?'

He had on a grey wool coat. Some of the buttons were broken on it. It was wrapped tightly round him against the cold. His skin was pock-marked, and he'd washed his hair so it frizzed around his temples. His brown eyes looked shyer than they had done before, apologetic almost.

'Can I come in?'

'No. I mean, no, let's go for a walk instead.'

'It's cold out here, you know.'

'I know, but I'd prefer to get some air.' I grabbed my coat

from the hallstand and closed the door quietly behind me. 'Just had to get out of there. Folks are driving me mad. You know how it is.'

'Of course,' he said, though he looked a little bewildered.

He was flicking his thumb nervously with his middle finger, over and over again, as if he was skimming stones. I looked back at the house as we got to the top of the driveway and could see Gran standing at the window. She must have hauled herself out of the chair when she heard the front door close. I just had to pray that she wouldn't say anything.

'I'm going to have a baby brother or sister soon.'

'What age is your mother?'

Here we were again, talking about mothers.

'I'm sorry.'

'What do you mean?'

'I mean, I don't know why I'm telling you . . . She's forty-four.'

He pulled a rotten stick from the ditch.

'That means she'll be drawing a pension when your little brother or sister is only twenty.'

'Suppose so. Do you have brothers or sisters?'

'No, I don't. I'm an only child.'

'So am I. Not for long, though – it's boring, isn't it?'

'Oh yes, terrible. I'd say my mother would have had more—'

'I'm sorry.'

'No, don't worry.'

We were headed for the cemetery, or rather he was leading me there.

'You ever been in that old cottage?'

'No. It looks dangerous.'

'It is,' he said. 'I like it. There're bats, you know. Come on.'

He took me by the hand and dragged me towards it. I was scared, but happy too that he was holding my hand. I would have liked Mar to see me then, being led into this secret place by my boyfriend. Or at least been able to tell her about it.

Once we'd clambered in over a broken wall at the back of the house, careful not to get stung or scratched by the nettles and brambles, Leon squeezed my hand even tighter so my fingers hurt. I'd started to sweat even though it was freezing cold. A starling fluttered out one of the windows. It felt as though we were further back from the road than we really were, away from the world. He pushed me, gently at first, against one of the moss-covered walls, holding me by my shoulders, kissing me hard. Then he pushed his whole weight onto me and I squirmed, but he wouldn't let me go. He was grappling with the buckle on my belt, and I pulled his hand away. I don't know why. It was what I wanted. But it didn't feel right there, just up the road from my house and so near the graveyard. Strands of my hair were catching in the rough surface of the wall and being woven into tiny knots and gently torn from my head. I was conscious of insects – dead flies caught in cobwebs sticking in my hair, beetles on the ground crawling near our feet. I could barely see Leon's face as I pulled it back from mine. His eyes were like pools of light reflected on a watery surface.

'Do you not like me?' he whispered.

'What do you mean?'

'Do I make you sick?'

'What are you on about?' He was frightening me. 'You know I like you.'

'Then why will you not kiss me? Why did you push me away?'

'I just wanted to look at you,' I said, peering into his eyes.

My own eyes were filling with tears. I wanted to get away, but if I tried to leave then he'd be sure I didn't like him. And I did. I wasn't lying when I said I wanted to look at him. I wanted to look in his eyes, see if I could fathom what was going on, if they could explain things. He held my face in his hands, wiping tears away with his thumbs. He kissed my eyelids, then my cheeks, then my lips. My head felt like porcelain.

There was a rustle in the grass just outside the cottage. We stood stock still, not even daring to blink. More rustling, then a scuttling noise as something came into the cottage, something small enough to squeeze through one of the gaps in the wall.

It was Blue. She yelped, and clawed at Leon's legs. He laughed.

'Well, if it isn't old Blue.'

'You remember her?'

'Yes, of course. Me and Blue are good friends. Aren't we, pup?' He patted her head roughly.

'Have you seen me here before, Leon?'

'I told you.'

'When?'

'I've been watching you. From your garden. Through your window.'

'What?'

'Your back garden.'

His voice had grown more faint even than before.

'What do you mean?'

He didn't answer.

'You've seen me?'

'Yes,' he whispered.

'I think I better go now.'

I fumbled my way past him in the dark, through the tall grass and brambles, through the window at the back of the cottage. He didn't try to stop me. I stung my hand on a nettle. It felt good, in a strange way.

I was relieved to be outside. He followed behind me, saying nothing. He seemed giddy, his hands fidgeting, his eyes darting in the darkness.

'I'm sorry.'

'I just need to get back.'

I loved him then, really loved him, though I couldn't for the life of me figure out why. Maybe because he'd seen me in my room, seen me undress, seen me naked – and wanted me, desired me. Because he'd waited until dark to walk down our driveway, hidden, probably behind the shed, and watched for the light in my room, and for me sitting at my desk, reading, doing my homework, getting ready for bed . . .

I panicked then. 'It was just you, wasn't it?'

'Yes, just me.'

I turned to look at him, took his hand in mine, and we walked the few minutes back to my house. I kissed him on the cheek and ran down the driveway, wondering if he'd wait until I was indoors before he crept down to the back of the house to spy on me.

꩜

'There you are,' Mam said as I blustered into the kitchen, Blue behind me. Specks of colour danced in front of my eyes.

'Dinner'll be ready in five minutes.'

She stopped what she was doing to look at me.

'You look nice.'

'Thanks,' I said, walking quickly to the hall doorway.

'Oh, before I forget, love, would you bring those glasses over to Mary. Go on over now before dinner's on the table, will you? She'll be lost without them.'

She pointed to them on the dining room table. I picked them up and headed out the back door again, wary of bumping into Leon as I turned the corner. But he was nowhere about, that I could see. Blue ran up onto the lawn ahead of me, sniffing furiously. I remembered that Gran had seen Leon, and that I would have to have a word with her after dinner.

My knickers felt damp.

Blue ran under my legs as we got to the top of the driveway, hesitated for a second as she saw the headlights of a car approaching, then made a dash for the other side of the road.

There was a dull thud and screech of brakes. The driver might have thought it was a badger, except for he saw me. I opened my mouth to scream but nothing came out. Mary appeared at her front door, hands white with flour held up above her head. She came running down their driveway.

'What in God's name? Are you okay, Lani? Oh Christ,' she said as she realised it was the dog and not me who'd been run over. She was wearing a pink gingham apron.

'I didn't see it,' the driver said. 'When I did it was too late.'

'Jesus,' Mary said, bending over Blue.

I turned my head away. I couldn't bear to look.

'We're going to have to carry her into the house.'

'I can't,' I said. That's all I could say – 'I can't.' I wouldn't. I didn't want to touch her.

'I'm very sorry,' the driver said.

Mary took the dog up in her arms as gently as she could, and we stumbled up to her house like we were both drunk. Paddy was standing at the front door.

'I've called Martin,' he said as we approached. 'He'll be here as soon as he can.'

I heard the car pull off.

'Here, put her in here on the couch. I've put some news-paper down.'

Why had he put papers down? They always let her sit on the couch. Why papers now? I couldn't fathom it. She wasn't mucky or bleeding.

They laid her down. She was very still. Just the slight heaving of her chest. And her eyes. Her eyes were darting frantically from side to side – not looking at me or Mary or Paddy, but at something else.

'Now, I'd better call your mother and father,' Paddy said.

'I'm supposed to be home for dinner.'

'It's okay, pet. Here, you sit over here,' said Mary.

She pointed to an armchair at the other side of the room.

'Can I get you anything?'

'No thanks. I need to go outside.'

My cheeks felt all numb, my jaw leaden. I kept having to swallow.

'Okay, love, well you can go out there into the front room if you'd prefer.'

She held my elbow lightly as we walked out into the hallway, as if I might topple over.

I was still holding her glasses. 'Oh, these are for you,' I said, holding them out to her. 'You forgot them – last night.'

I wished I hadn't said that then.

'Oh God,' she said. 'Thanks, Lani. I'm so sorry . . . I—'

The hallway was cold. It smelled of wax polish. The old-fashioned lights on the walls gave off a drab light, the maroon-and-white flocked wallpaper was speckled with black mould just above the hall table. There was a green telephone and an open address book. Probably Mary had been organising the next game of golf with the girls, or calling one of her sisters. And now she had a dying dog on her couch.

Headlights shone through the windows by the front door and swung round to the side of the house. Car doors slammed – one, two – and the back door of the house was pushed open. They were whispering, Mam and Dad, and Paddy and Mary. Not whispering exactly, but talking very quietly, slowly, trying to make sense of things. Their old dog. She was still breathing, but there was no sign of Martin. Off putting someone's pet hamster to sleep, probably. I saw Mam crouch down beside Blue, stroking her head very gently. I was relieved she was there to take care of things. Blue would understand – wouldn't she? – how I couldn't bear to be near her. I counted the wooden tiles on the hall floor. I wondered if Paddy had put those tiles down himself, or if someone had come in to do it for him. I wondered if Leon was in our back garden and, if he was, what he was making of all of this. Dad was walking towards me. I don't know what that look on his face was. I'd never seen it before.

'Where's Gran?' I asked.

'She's dozing, love. We thought we'd leave her there, not disturb her.'

'But what if . . .'

I couldn't say it. He put his arm around my shoulders;

I could feel the warmth of his palm, the pressure of the pads of his fingers.

'Ah God, she's wet the couch,' Mam said.

'Don't worry, Deirdre. Don't worry.'

Their voices were underwater-sounding. This is all happening very quickly, I was thinking. Because it was. It's surprising how quickly these things happen – how suddenly time rushes ahead of itself. How much time had passed? Maybe fifteen minutes? Where is that driver now? Now Blue is soiling the furniture.

Dad was still gripping my shoulder. We stood, facing somewhere between the door to the living room and the hall table. The swoosh of tyres on the driveway again. It was Martin in his green Land Rover that smelled of cow dung and iodine.

I remembered being out on a farm with him and Mam, seeing lambs have their tails cut by the farmer, the screeching noise they made, and the drops of blood as they stumbled from between his knees.

Martin entered by the back door too.

'Well, let's have a look at her,' he said, lifting Mam gently up and settling down to inspect the damage.

'Looks like she's broken her back, I'm afraid. Not much we can do. I can put her to sleep. Are you happy for me to do that?'

He glanced first at Mam, then at Dad and me in the hallway. Mam was white as a sheet, biting the skin around one of her fingers, trying not to cry. She nodded, Dad nodded. I stared at him, thinking how 'broken back' makes a sound like splitting bark. I didn't realise I had to answer.

'Lani?'

'Oh yes, that's fine,' I said, as if I'd been asked if that was enough milk in my tea, and tell me when to stop. Dad squeezed my shoulder. Mam was standing directly under the light in the living room, a halo around her tilted head making her look like a female Francis of Assisi or Padre Pio or who was it, with her childish pot belly.

'Right so,' said Martin. 'It'll be completely painless for wee Blue, here. Over very quickly. Deirdre, would you like to stay and pet her so she's not frightened?'

It was too late for that: she was scared out of her wits, nothing moving but those darting, frightened eyes. Couldn't they see that? I walked slowly into the room, knelt down beside her and gently rubbed, with one finger, the soft fur between those eyes. She felt surprisingly warm. We held each other's gaze for a few seconds, and I could have sworn her panting slowed, but that could have been her heart counting down, unwinding. Then her eyes rolled back in her head and I could see the white of them and nothing else. There were little white patches of flour on her coat. Mam put her hand on my shoulder, saying 'The sooner this is over—'

My knees cracked as I stood up. Dad, Paddy and Mary followed me into the hallway, and from there into the front room, where Mary had put the gas fire on. It felt as if that room hadn't been heated in months. It smelt of damp, and the dust burning on the metal bars of the fire.

'I'll go and make us all a nice cup of tea in a minute,' Mary said.

In a few minutes Blue would be dead, and we could have tea and biscuits. I was hungry. Tea and biscuits seemed like a good idea.

No one said a word after that, not until we heard the door of the living room open and Mam's footsteps on the wooden floor of the hallway, and her sobbing uncontrollably. They all rose from their seats at once and hovered around Mam at the door, Dad taking her in his arms and rubbing the back of her head protectively, saying '*I know, I know,*' and Mary saying 'A nice cup of tea – that's what you need. Tea with sugar: it's great for shock.'

She looked embarrassed. I remembered again why I'd come over that evening, and I wanted to remind her. I hated them then, Mam and Mary. All of them. If they hadn't been playing their stupid cards the night before, and if Mary hadn't gotten drunk and forgotten her glasses, and if Mam hadn't insisted that I bring them over that evening, Blue wouldn't be dead.

It was my fault. I knew that. I should have had a hold of her collar. Mam sat on the arm of my chair. She was shaking, just as I was.

'Are you okay, pet?' she asked, stroking the back of my neck.

Leon's hand had been there not so long before. Maybe she'd smell him.

'Mary's getting us some tea.'

I know, I wanted to say, I'm not deaf. But I said nothing.

Martin came into the room, his hands clasped. 'I'm very sorry.'

'Oh no, thank you, Martin,' Mam said. 'You did everything you could. Now, would you stay for a cup of tea?'

'Oh, yes, that'd be lovely.' He paused. 'Do you want me to take her with me?'

'No,' I said, and everyone looked at me. 'We'll be burying her in our garden.'

'Fair enough. Fair enough. I've left her in the garage out the back.'

'Thanks, Martin,' Dad said. 'I'll take her down to ours.'

Blue was almost drowned as a pup. It was Dad who rescued her. He didn't even ask Mam if she'd mind. Just arrived home with her one Saturday afternoon when Mam thought he'd been into the hardware store in town. We called her Blue because her fur was so black it looked blue in a certain light. And because one of Mam's favourite songs was 'Old Blue', that one Joan Baez used to sing about the dog.

Mary carried in a large tray with cups, milk jug, teapot, a plate of biscuits and even some sandwiches she'd somehow managed to rustle up.

'Jesus, that's lovely, Mary. Just what we all need,' said Paddy.

His tongue made a clicking noise as he spoke, sticking to the roof of his mouth. My mouth was dry too – terribly dry. There was a foul taste at the back of my throat, the past few hours turned sour. The taste of Leon's tongue – the watery, sweet taste – had gone.

There was a smell of sweat from Mam's armpits, like cat piss. Sister Anne wouldn't have been impressed, I thought. Sandwiches and biscuits were passed round as Mary poured our tea – strong black tea – into maroon glazed cups.

'Sugar?' She looked around the room. 'Shall I just put sugar in all of them? We could do with it.'

'Yes, that'd be grand, Mary,' said Martin.

'Yes, lovely,' said Mam.

None of the rest of us objected.

'That road's awful dangerous,' Paddy said.

'Just as long as it's none of us.'

'With the help of God,' Mary said.

Mary had just got back from Lough Derg, praying from dawn till dusk. To save us all. Or just to save herself. It was no wonder she got so drunk the night before. She was skin and bones. I half-expected her to get down on her knees and start decades of the rosary, but then I reminded myself that Blue was just a dog.

My tea was a little stronger than I would have liked – so strong it left me with more of a thirst than I'd started with, left a kind of starchiness on my tongue. I wasn't used to it sweet either. It made things seem even more odd.

Dad had to put his whole weight onto the spade to dig into the stony soil in the back garden. I pulled tufts of long yellow grass out of his way. We put plastic sheeting into the hole. I don't know why, but we did, and then Dad laid Blue down and we covered her over with compost and soil. I wanted a little compost, to be sure forget-me-nots would grow in the spring.

＊ ＊

My darling Lani,

I didn't mean to frighten you. I have been up half the night
wondering what to write to you, and now it is four in the
morning, and the dormitory is eerily quiet. I wish I hadn't told
you that I've been watching you, but then I couldn't lie to you.
I have seen you. I have seen your naked flesh. And the thought
of it makes me burn — with shame and excitement.

I hope you will forgive me. You were very quiet when
I left. I'd hate to think that I've caused you any pain. I've
never felt this way about anybody. To think that I may have
brought this to an end before it has even begun is too unbearable
to contemplate.

Do you feel like I do? The desperation, the unravelling? I
wanted to tear you open, tear myself open. I wanted to crawl
into you. I wanted you to hurt me. It does hurt so much, this
constant yearning to be with you, inside you.

I'm sorry. I'm satisfied just to look until you're ready. I'm a skilled watcher. I know how to let time wash over me, to let everything else slip into oblivion.

I did feel that you wanted me — the heat of your body. Was I wrong? I don't know why I asked you if you found me repugnant. God knows, I wouldn't have wanted you to say so if you did. I just find it so difficult to believe that you, the one I have longed for all this time, have come to me, just like in my dream. It makes me so happy. YOU make me so happy. You have no idea.

I'm going home for Christmas, but can I see you before then? If I don't hear from you I'll know that you've decided that you want nothing more to do with me. I hope this isn't the case, but if it is I'll respect your wishes and stay out of your way.

Forever yours,

L.B.

The sky was the colour of eggshell, the path running down the middle of the graveyard slippery with black ice. I folded the letter, which I'd read over and over, so that it fitted in my fist and put it in the zipped pocket of my coat.

I made the sign of the cross before the pale, pink-flecked marble headstone.

In Loving Memory of
HERMIONE BRADY
1946–1983
She leaves behind her husband
and loving son
May She Rest In Peace

May her soul and the souls of all the faithfully departed rest in peace, I said to myself. It seemed only right.

He wanted to crawl into me.

He wanted me to *hurt* him.

That little boy, deserted by his mother. It must have felt like desertion – how else could he have understood it? That was why he watched me, so that I wouldn't slip away as she had. Watched me as the granite cherub on the grave next to his mother's did.

Paddy was out the front of his house, raking gravel. The tyre tracks from Martin's car were still there. Paddy held one hand over his forehead to shield his eyes from the glare of the sun and waved down to me with the other, mouthing hello, though all I could hear was a kind of whinnying sound, with the wind blowing.

Dad was down on his knees in the dirt of the flowerbed at the front of the house, tugging moss from between clumps of rock and heather, his large hands purple with the cold.

I walked around to the back of the house. The shed door was open, creaking rustily on one broken hinge. The poinsettias I'd put on Blue's grave were starting to wither already. I'd picked them up at the florist's while Mam was buying a Christmas wreath for the front door and telling the florist all about Blue, and the florist saying 'Ah God, that's awful,' and 'God help us,' and looking over at me. I couldn't think what else to get: it was too early for forget-me-nots and I thought poinsettias would look pretty if it snowed.

I'd had to carry Blue home from the fields at the back of the house many times over the years – her fur clotted with snow, packed hard, layer upon layer, so that she couldn't walk anymore.

The ice on the tall grass around the grave was thawing in the faint sunlight, saturating the legs of my trousers and my shoes. I crouched down, clutching one hand in the other for warmth.

'I'm sorry I let you die, Blue. I'm sorry I didn't hold on to you, take better care of you.'

I pictured her frozen hard in the ground, her eyes wide open.

The air in the kitchen was oily with the smells of the morning's fry. Mam was upstairs sleeping. I went about clearing the table, wiping it down, filling the basin with hot sudsy water. Ordinarily I hated washing up, but I didn't mind it so much that afternoon. It helped take my mind off things, and the sun was shining directly in through the window above the sink, onto the top of my head.

When I'd finished I put my hand up to feel my hair and it felt like hot ironed silk. I went into the front room to see if Gran wanted anything. I thought I'd better.

She was reading the obituaries in the local paper.

꩜

Dearest Leon,

You did frighten me a little, but you mustn't worry. I haven't ever felt this way about anyone either, and I don't want it to end. I won't leave you, my darling. And I don't want to hurt you. I've no intention of it.

I have bad news, I'm afraid. Just after you left the other night I was going across the road when Blue ran out in front of me and was hit by a car. I know how much you and her got on. It's been awful here since. Everyone's so upset. I've made her a grave in our garden, marked by a circle of stones.

I think about you every minute of every day. I look out my window at night, wondering if you're watching me. I feel as though you are.

Write to me soon. Please?

Love,

Lani

He turned up unexpectedly a few days later. I was out getting coal. I felt a hand on my shoulder and my heart freeze in my chest. In my dreams I roll over at the first sign of trouble, belly-up, just waiting to be killed. But that's not how this went. I felt a cold fire crackle through my veins and swung round, bucket in one hand, cold steel shovel in the other, and caught the corner of his jaw with its blunt edge. He reached up to press his hand against the hurt.

'You scared the life out of me,' I said.

'And *you*'ve just nearly broken my jaw.'

He didn't flinch as I pulled his hand away from his face to touch his purpling jaw and feel his warm blood between my fingers.

'You're bleeding,' I whispered.

'It doesn't matter. Listen, Lani, I'm sorry. Sorry I frightened you. I only wanted to say how sorry I was. Sorry about

Blue . . .' He sounded strange, couldn't open his mouth properly to talk. He pulled me to him.

'I don't ever want you to let go of me.'

'I won't,' he said, and it felt as though he meant it. I *won't*.

He didn't stay long. He had to be back at the school before they noticed him gone. But the time he did stay, there was no one and nothing else in the world, and though I felt a keen sadness – palpable almost – I was also serenely happy.

He told me he would keep me close, always. He told me he would watch over me.

I told him I was his girl.

Deirdre, 8

I had special shoes my mammy bought me. Special shoes and a ribbon for my hair, and my mammy said that I was a great girl and that I would be a champion Irish dancer one day. I was doing it every day. I do it every day here, out in the yard. Jump threes, hop threes, side steps. Mother Carmel beats me if she sees me doing it wrong, so I try not to, but sometimes I make a mistake by accident.

My daddy was a man with no backbone. That's what my mammy told me. I never saw him myself. He must've looked queer. He probably walked like Old Peter, who was bent over so far he talked to the floor. Old Peter came around every day and my mammy would always give him a cup of tea and some bread. His head would be almost touching the table. I liked watching him trying to eat, like he was a dog. Sometimes I felt sorry for him. But most of the time I'd just be practising my hop threes.

The father of Jack, my youngest brother, would come around as well, and I used to want him to be my father as well, instead of the man with no backbone who never even came to see me. He panted a lot when we were all in bed, me and Jack and the other wee ones. Panted and grunted. He must have been thinking we were all asleep. But none of us were. We were laughing under the blanket. It sounded like he was going to the toilet for a long time.

One time I came home from school and Mammy was lying on the floor in the kitchen. There was a smell of chicken giblets. It looked like she'd been lying there so long she got hungry and decided to eat her own tongue. The baby was roaring crying.

She just had a funny turn, that's all. Me and my brothers and sisters are all going back when she gets better. Jack's daddy said he would look after her, and I promised him I would look after my sisters, but I'm not really allowed to talk to them.

I won a silver medal for Irish dancing at the Feis and the nuns made me give it to them to make a crown for the statue of Our Lady. When I win the gold medal I will take it home and give it to my mammy, and she will make me brown bread and jam and butter to celebrate.

Mar was Tinkerbell in the Christmas pantomime and Eoin was Peter Pan. They were a right pair.

I was working on the stage scenery and was sick to the back teeth of seeing them snogging backstage. They weren't exactly discreet – they didn't care who saw them. Every opportunity they got, her in her ballet skirt, him in his green tights. They'd gone all the way, apparently. The whole school seemed to know about it.

She was becoming like all the other girls – enveloped in a thick fog of fag smoke, cheap talk and soap operas. Not light as air like I was with knowing I had found the love of my life. Not made up of glass splinters reflecting the light, like I was. I'd no need to daydream anymore, even. I could will myself into a trance-like state where I *embodied* Leon. I took on his form, and he mine.

One of the days, after rehearsal, Mar was there outside the school with her actor-friends, smoking away. I didn't look over at them – they were from the year above, most of those girls, and they hadn't said two words to me since we'd started rehearsals except to tell me if I'd done something wrong or to boss me about. I could feel all of them looking at me, though. I made my eyes go all yolky round the edges so all I could see was the door to the school ahead of me.

'How's your *Addams Family* freak?' one called after me, the others humming the theme tune.

Shrieks of laughter followed me down the pale green corridor, with its white and dark-blue tiles and eggy smells from the science labs. The laughter sounded further away than it really was. I could do that special thing with my hearing as well, so that everything went fuzzy round the edges, like I was sitting at the bottom of a swimming pool. Only afterwards I'd get a high-pitched ringing in them, which I couldn't make go away. It carried on for most of that day.

The girls were up on the desks in the classroom, with their skirts rolled up round their thighs, their blouses tied in knots round their waists, swaggering up and down a makeshift catwalk.

'Get up here, you,' someone shouted at me. 'It's a slag competition!' and she pulled her skirt a little further up, snaking her hips.

I turned round, flung up my skirt and flashed my well-covered backside, which rose whoops from the girls. It was easier to do that than nothing. Josephine was sitting crimsonly at the front of the room – her and some of the quieter girls – pretending to look for something in her bag by her feet. Then Mar came in behind me, jumped up on one of the desks and started to undress, very slowly. The girls roared with laughter and excitement, and started shouting. 'Get your kit off! Show us your tits! Strip! Strip! Strip!'

Mr Davis walked in. 'What's gotten into you, Marjorie Halpern?'

'Nothing, sir,' Mar said, climbing down off the desk and buttoning up her blouse slowly and seductively, biting her lower lip as she did so, and all the time looking him right in the eye, which gave all the other girls time to get back to their seats.

He blushed. 'Enough of this nonsense now.'

The room smelled of something strange.

Outside later, Mar came at me with a bag of white flour. It caught me hard on the shoulder blade and burst all over my clothes. I wasn't supposed to get upset, it was supposed to be for laughs, all the girls were doing it, what was wrong with me. But I couldn't stop myself from crying.

I slumped onto the footpath. Mar sat down beside me.

'I'm sorry. Christ. Since when did you get so touchy?'

She wasn't helping.

'Look, Lane, I'm sorry, okay? But you've been acting really weird lately.'

'Yeah, well, my dog just died.'

'Blue? Why didn't you say?'

Her telling me that she'd had at least three cats killed on

the road wasn't any use. You couldn't compare Blue with some mangy old cats from off her farm.

'What were those girls on about earlier?' I sniffed.

'Oh, they were just trying to be funny. About Leon. You know.'

'No, I don't know.'

'You know. About his father.'

'*No!*' I shouted, snot bubbling from my nose. 'What are you talking about?'

A man had killed his wife. Years ago. When we were kids. Remember? A man had killed his wife. And the man was home. He wasn't locked up. He was home, looking after his son. It was all over the papers. And it was all people talked about for years. And didn't I remember? Didn't I know? I *must* have known. She thought I knew. And all the girls at school thought I knew. And they were all laughing at me. He lived with his psycho father. And wouldn't my parents have talked about it? Someone should have told me. *She* should have told me. He should have. Why was I the only one? Killed her one night. It was all over the papers.

I slapped her hard in the face.

'You're sick,' was all she said, before getting up and walking off and leaving me there alone.

I puked behind the shed, wiped my mouth on my sleeve, and went to biology class.

Sylvia sneered at me as I went to sit down in the only free seat left, next to her, and Mar elbowed her in the ribs and whispered at her to keep her gob shut.

'Are you okay, Lani?' the teacher asked.

'I'm fine, Miss,' I said, resenting her for drawing attention to me.

'Right. Well, today we're talking about photosynthesis.' She tapped her chalk on the blackboard.

I was having to gulp really hard to stop the tears from coming, but I couldn't stop them.

I ran from the class.

No one came after me.

CR

I found Leon's father's number in the phone book. Stephen Brady, his name was. I knew Leon was still at school, but I wanted to hear his father's voice. The phone rang for a long time. I was just about to put it down when he answered. He spoke very quietly, almost inaudibly.

'Hello?'

'Hello, could I speak to Leon please?' My voice was shaking a little.

He hesitated, inhaled deeply, said something indecipherable under his breath.

'That boy isn't here. I don't know where he is. He never is—'

'He never is?'

'He's outside, I think. He's gone somewhere.'

'Can you tell him I called?'

'Yes, I'll tell him.'

I waited for him to ask who I was, but he didn't.

'I'm Lani.'

'Does he know who you are?'

'Yes, he does. My name's Lani Devine.'

He hung up.

I tried to call Leon's school, but no one answered.

I tried to write to him, but I just ended up writing his name over and over again until the paper was scratched through.

CR

The last day before the holidays we were ushered to confession in the old convent part of the school. There was a special room there that smelled of cabbage and incense and old carpet. As usual I told the priest it was two months since my last confession, that I had not loved God, etcetera, and then asked him if it was okay to love someone who had committed a mortal sin.

'Love thy neighbour as thyself,' he answered.

'But what if thy neighbour's a murdering—' I stopped myself.

'He who casts the first stone . . .' he went on.

He wasn't listening.

He said mass after that, and we all filed up for communion. He placed the wafer on my tongue, then his hand on my forehead, very slowly, as if I was the chosen one or something. At the end of mass we sang 'Knocking on Heaven's Door' out of tune.

The girls were acting all stupid backstage that night. It was like they didn't see me when they looked at me. Some of them even smiled. But it wasn't at me. More like their reflection in my eyes.

Mr Breslin was running around like a blue-arsed fly. 'Where in God's name is my Peter Pan?'

I was having to do some of the make-up because the girls were too nervous. It was hard to make them stay still while I plastered their faces with gloopy stage paint. Mar was fidgeting up and down on the spot, like she was warming up before a race. Eoin swaggered in late, looking all cool.

'Hi, Lani,' he said, speaking to me for the first time. 'Leon's here.'

I felt sick to my stomach. I peered out at the audience. Leon was sitting two rows behind my parents.

The whole time I was standing behind the curtains, opening and closing them for different scenes, I watched him. He didn't look any different, now I knew. He didn't look anything, except maybe a little amused. It occurred to me that maybe he was just as cold and calculating as his father.

He came backstage afterwards, clapped Eoin on the back, told him he looked like a right ponce in his girlie tights, and the two of them laughed. I'd never seen him like that before. Then he walked over to me.

I didn't move.

'You look like you've seen a ghost,' he said. 'It's only me. Have you got stage fright?'

'I don't want you anywhere near me,' I said, my throat going all tight.

He didn't say anything. He just turned and walked away, with everyone there watching.

I had no idea that was what would come out of my mouth. It was like someone else had spoken.

I couldn't sleep that night.

The next day I went to the library in town after school and found the story in the local newspaper archive, 27 December 1983:

> ### TRAGIC DEATH OF WOMAN IN CROGHER
> A young woman from Crogher has died from multiple stab wounds, leaving her family devastated and a community in shock. She was rushed to the General Hospital late on Christmas Day. It is believed that her husband alerted the Gardaí. She was declared dead upon arrival. The Gardaí do not wish to comment at this stage, pending further investigation.

There was another account in the same paper a week later, along with a picture of a blue-eyed, blonde-haired beauty queen — that's what she looked like. She was younger in the picture than she would have been when she was killed, maybe twenty only. She was smiling.

HUSBAND HELD OVER WIFE'S DEATH

Stephen Brady has been arrested on suspicion of the murder of his wife, Hermione Brady, late on Christmas Day. Stephen and Hermione Brady had been married for eight years, and had one child together. People in the community are shocked. One man commented: 'Stephen Brady was a sound man. I never heard a bad word said against him, and I worked with him for many years.' Mr Brady has worked at the bank in Crogher for over twenty years. He met his wife when she first moved there from England, and they married shortly afterwards.

Teachers and neighbours alike were unanimous in their praise of the family. Of their son, one teacher commented, 'He's a happy, bright boy.' 'There was never a bother on him,' another said. According to one neighbour, Mrs Brady was 'a lovely, cheerful girl'.

Mr Brady is said to have given himself up to the Gardaí on the same night. He is currently being held in the county station.

I don't know how long I stayed staring at those articles, and at that picture. Her, smiling. She had a small mouth, I remember thinking, small teeth. And a high forehead and expressive eyes, as if there was nothing she could possibly have to hide. I searched for a likeness to Leon. It was there – in that certain way her head was tilted, the flare of the nostrils – subtle as anything, but it was there. I folded the papers away, put them back on the shelf and walked quickly out of the library.

I went straight up to the graveyard that evening, and to Hermione's grave. It was freezing cold – too cold to hang around for long – but I was there long enough to say some kind of prayer for her, and to tell her I would look after Leon. Then I went home and wrote a note to him. 'I love you,' is what it said, 'and I'm sorry.'

That night I dreamt I was in a dirty bed. The sheets and pillowcases were a greyish-yellow, and thrown over them was an oil sheet, like I'd had as a child. I didn't have any clothes on and it was cold. A large man, larger than I'd ever seen in real life, crawled into the bed beside me. He was very familiar. I knew him: I'm not sure how, it might have been the smell of him. He pushed me down into the bed – down, down.

It went on for a long time, and there wasn't anything I could do to stop it. When he was gone I floated up off the bed. I was floating, looking down, and I could see blood on the sheets. My stomach hurt. I woke early in the morning with cramp.

Aisling, 11

I eat the chickens' food sometimes. I'm always starving. Worse than all the other girls. Denise says it's because I grow so quick. I'm only eleven but I'm taller than her, and she is twelve. I grow out of my dresses really fast but I have to wear them anyway with the sleeves biting into my armpits. It's hard to breathe sometimes they get so tight. I bring tea up to Peter in the garden sometimes and he gives me a tomato, or a handful of raspberries if they're ripe. Sometimes even a carrot. Carrots can make you see in the dark if you eat enough of them. When no one is looking I go to where they put the scraps for the chickens and I pick out the best bits. Carrot and turnip skins are the best. But sometimes I'll have potato peelings as well, if there is nothing else. I scrape the dirt off them and keep them for the night and eat them in bed. If it's a nice taste, like carrot or turnip, I'll suck on it for a while before I eat it.

Denise thinks I don't know what's going on with her and Mother Assumpta but I do. I'm not thick. Denise says I am too quiet but I'm not. I just don't want to get in trouble. I like it when it's the nuns' retreat and we have to be quiet for a whole three days before Christmas. All you can hear is the babies crying because you can't make them quiet like you can the bigger girls.

I am in charge of the toilets for the small girls. I have to make sure they don't make any mess. If they do I get in trouble so I am very strict with them.

Denise doesn't remember her parents but I remember mine. My mammy was the prettiest woman I ever seen. She had blue eyes and blonde hair and she used to make me cakes all the time. I don't know what happened her.

There is this townie girl who brings in rhubarb and sugar to school and gives it to me and some of the other girls. I think her mother must be like mine. We don't show the teacher or we would get in trouble. We sneak it outside in the yard when the girls are playing hoop.

I get a pain in my tummy sometimes when I eat the potato skins but not the rhubarb. It is delicious. And sometimes I get a pain that goes all the way from my tummy to my neck. It is because I am growing too fast. I am being stretched. It feels like there is a big hole in the middle that is always empty.

❧

We had Mary and Paddy over for drinks that Christmas Eve, as we always did. Mam made mulled wine and laid the mince pies out on paper doilies on china plates. Mam wasn't feeling too well so they had to go home early. I stayed up watching telly with Gran. She fell asleep with her wine glass tilted in her hand.

Christmas morning I was up early so I could help get the dinner ready. Dad lit a fire in the front room with damp mossy logs that hissed in the grate. The house smelled of hot fruit and pine needles. We brought Mam breakfast in bed.

It was Dad's birthday, but he never liked any fuss, so it was no different that year from any other. We just gave him a card and a silk tie, same as he always got. He opened it sitting on the bed while Mam picked at her food.

'Thanks, love,' he said, leaning over to kiss her on the forehead. 'Thanks, Lani,' he said, stretching over to me on the other side of the bed and kissing me too.

By early afternoon everyone was sat in front of the television in paper hats. We'd been to half-eleven mass, visited the Reillys for drinks, exchanged gifts by the tree in the front room, and eaten our overcooked roast turkey. Its skin was chewier than it should have been, and the dark meat around the legs tore from the bones in strips. We didn't go in for all the frills that year, what with Mam being under the weather.

I crept out the back door, put some holly on Blue's grave and headed up to the cemetery. I was sure Leon would be there. I wanted to see him more than anything.

I walked to the top of the graveyard and, minding not to tear my clothes, climbed through a small hole in the whitethorn hedge that Blue used to use and crouched down. It was bitterly cold and starting to sleet. The field was empty, which I was glad of: cows frightened me when they got too close.

I could see clear enough through the tangle of weed and thorn.

I didn't ever doubt that he would come just then, just as I wanted him to. I waited long enough that my knees were starting to ache and my hands and wrists were hurting from the cold, when I heard the familiar crunch of car wheels on the gravel in the car park. But it wasn't Leon. My ears were stinging. The car pulled away and I was out through the hole in the hedge and about to ramble down the path, just to stretch my limbs for a minute, when I heard another car sweeping over the stones. I scrambled back to the ditch, ducking so I wouldn't be seen, and scraped through again, ripping tiny slivers of skin on the thorns. It barely hurt, my hands were that numb, but I could see little threads of blood along my thumb on one hand, and from thumb to wrist on the other.

It was sleeting heavily then. I didn't have a hat or a hood, but I couldn't leave.

It was them, Leon and his father. They walked to the grave. His father's body seemed to cave in on itself, and Leon put one arm under his to support him. He had an umbrella in his other hand, which he held more over the father than himself. Leon looked up suddenly, in my direction, and my foot slipped as I ducked a little further, though I knew there was no way he could see me. Maybe he expected to. He was taller than his father, broader across the shoulders. He looked strong beside him, more handsome than I remembered, with his face beaded in water and wisps of hair sticking to his skin. I wanted him to see me. I wanted him to let go of that wicked old man and come to me. I didn't like that man touching him.

The hem of my coat was smeared with mud, and my hair was soaked right through. Water was seeping into the collar of my blouse and down my back. I skulked along the hedgerow to the back of the Reillys' garden, and Mrs Sheridan's beside them, and turned down the tractor trail that led to the road, opposite our house. I'm still not sure what I was going to do. I might have thought that I could walk around and meet them just as they were coming away from the grave. And then what, I don't know. My shoes squelched in the pocked grass. Mrs Sheridan stood in her kitchen looking out through a little porthole she'd rubbed in the steamed window. She was probably saving the scraps of her leftover Christmas dinner in Tupperware boxes for the next day. Mam's pudding would be in the microwave. I didn't know whether to wave or not. I chose to walk on, pretending I hadn't seen her.

Their car drove past just as I got to the top of our driveway. Then I saw that it was Leon driving. The windscreen wipers swept the sleet away from his face, then blurred it again seconds later. Though I'm sure he saw me – how could he not, me standing there bedraggled, with my clothes all muddy? – he didn't let on.

His father was sitting in the back seat gazing over towards my house. I felt ashamed of myself then, and appalled at the same time – that I'd crouched down in a ditch and spied on these people, and that this murderer was peering into my home. I wished the hedgerow was higher so he couldn't see in. It felt like Leon was playing some kind of sick joke. The whole thing was a sick joke. He was a liar. How could I believe anything? But the thing my mind kept turning back to, funnily, was that Leon could drive. It seemed so odd. I'm not sure why.

Sometimes I found it hard to walk back into that house of ours. It was always so quiet, even when Mam and Dad and Gran were there. It was a lonely place to step back into. It was worse after Blue. But I was glad that day. The house was warm for once. Every room was warm, even the hallway. I changed out of my wet clothes, plucking little tokens of grass and black twig from my skin and hair, and wrapped a fresh dry towel around my head. I washed the dried blood from my hands. With a needle I got from Mam's sewing basket I painstakingly removed a small thorn that had lodged itself deep in the soft cushion of flesh at the base of my left thumb. I liked the unflinching pain, the self-inflicted pain that was so unsurprising. And afterwards the emptiness in my head, and the feel of the cold wooden floor on my bare feet, and then the warmth of the fire and the soft carpet in the front room. They were all dozing. I sat close to Mam on the settee, close enough that I could feel the rise and fall of her. *The Sound of Music* was on the telly.

I played it over and over in my head. The Child of Prague in the window. That dark house. His quiet steps as he climbed the stairs to his son's room. The pretty blonde lady sleeping in bed. Him downstairs preparing, before the steps, before the lights went out, before his son slept. His whole body shaking. Her screeching. Like foxes out in the dark. The neighbours' light going on. The sound of the knife in her skin. The puncturing. His face all lit up with hate. The little boy sleeping. His sweet little face. Blood on the bedclothes and on the carpet. His father tucking him in, saying *It's all right now, son, it's only a bad dream.* And his heavy eyelids drooping again. Her body on the floor, slumped on her front, like she was sunbathing or sleeping. A bubble of spit at the corner of her mouth. Her eyes set on something in the distance. The way the guards must have crouched down by the body, crossed themselves. Avoided making eye contact with the dead woman. And the ambulance men taking her away. The boy on the landing being hushed into a spare bedroom. Their silence. Leon boiling potatoes for his father. His father saying *He never is.*

CR

Mam and I were sitting at the kitchen table on St Stephen's Day morning when it started to snow. Dad had been saying it would for days – standing at the window, saying it'll snow all right, sure look at that sky. He loved it to snow on his birthday. It was like God letting him know he hadn't forgotten, sending him the one thing he loved more than most. It didn't matter that it was a day late.

'Would you look?' he said, beaming. 'What did I tell you?'

We watched the big flakes falling slowly from the sky, sticking to the roof of the shed, the string of clematis branches outside the window, the frozen grass. Mam had her feet up on the chair to relieve her swollen ankles. I sipped my third cup of tea of the morning. Dad leaned on the sill, peering out.

'I'm going out in it,' he said, and I watched him from the window a few minutes later, his smoky breath in the cold, the flakes sticking to his hair, and him clapping his gloved hands together, everything muffled.

'Do you know, I must ring that brother of mine,' Mam said, lifting her legs wearily from the chair and heaving herself up. 'I haven't even told him the good news.'

She was slow to walk to the phone, leaf through the address book for his number and pick up the receiver. Reluctant, almost.

'Hello, could I speak to Father Patrick please?'

'Hello, Pat love. How are you? – Happy Christmas to you – good, good – God, that's great – Did you? – No, not at all – mmmm – Now listen here, love. You won't believe it, but I'm going to have a baby – Sure, I know – What? – Oh, yes – *What?*'

Her voice was shaking.

'You should have told me! When? – What did she say? – Have you got the address? – Okay, hold on till I get a pen.'

She held the phone between her ear and shoulder while she went through all the pens on the table, scribbling, scratching into the paper until she found one that worked.

'Got one – Right . . . Yes . . . Right so – No, no – Okay. I understand. You're a busy man – I will, I will. Okay. Bye.'

'What's the matter, Mam?'

She handed me the piece of paper she'd been scribbling on.

'What's this? Was he not happy about the baby?'

I looked at the name on it: 'Celia', scrawled over and over and an address somewhere in England.

'He only went and met her.'

'What?' I said, putting my hand on her shoulder.

'He went and met her without me. After me pleading with him for years to find her for me and him putting me off. The fucking bollocks.'

I'd never heard her use language like that before. She had begged him to help her. He was a priest, for God's sake, he must have access to records. A little girl orphaned out from the convent in town, it couldn't be that difficult to find her. But he said the records were destroyed in the fire that time, said there was no way of finding out. And the only other two people who might know were long dead.

'He fucking knew where she was. He knew everything . . .' she said, her eyes welling up with tears. 'Why would he keep that from me? For Jesus' sake, Mammy was only a child herself when Celia was born . . . Why couldn't he accept that? And now he fucking goes and sees her without me.'

Grandpa hadn't wanted them to have anything to do with Celia. A shame best kept hid, forgotten about. Uncle Patrick was no different.

She was shaking. I squeezed her hand in mine, told her to sit down.

'Didn't you know where she was? Didn't you know she was in Oxford?'

'Only just recently, when I got that book . . . And I

couldn't figure out how she'd tracked me down . . . But he *told me* it was best left alone. He *told me* she wouldn't want anything to do with us. And I was stupid enough to go along with him. But sure he must have given her the address . . .'

I couldn't help thinking that she *was* a bit stupid. If it was me and I knew I had a sister, I'd have been everywhere looking for her. Down at the convent, or wherever it was they kept records, trying to find out where she was. And especially after she got the book and knew for certain she was in Oxford. All she had to do was look in a phone book. I wouldn't have cared what my stupid brother thought. Just because he was a priest . . .

'God, Lani, I just felt something,' she said, putting her hand on her belly.

'I'll get Dad,' I said, running out of the room.

He was round at the front porch, leaning against the wall with both hands, belting the heels of his shoes on the footpath to remove the snow and ice.

'Would you look at that, Lani? The place'll be covered in no time at all.'

'Dad, the baby's kicking.'

It was like a prod with a cattle stick. He grabbed my arm, looked at me agog, and skidded down the hallway, leaving a trail of water on the parquet floor.

They were hugging each other when I put my head round the door.

'Is it okay if I come in?'

'Of *course* it is, love.'

It was like the fluttering of butterfly wings, she said. Only she could feel it. Dad had felt nothing. She was rosy-cheeked, tears streaming down her face. I couldn't bear to see her like that.

CR

Gran and Felim O'Rourke had known each other to see, Gran told me. I don't know what prompted her exactly. I suppose she could see I wasn't right, maybe she recognised something of herself in me. And sure with all the talk of the baby just then . . .

She and Felim had been practically neighbours, their houses only a couple of fields apart. And their fathers fished together the odd time, and shared a fondness for the drink. Felim helped her with the milk churns one day. He was passing on his bike and saw her struggling to lift them up onto the cart, the milk slopping over the sides and onto her skirt. He dismounted and helped her lift them before her father returned, saying a lady like her shouldn't be doing a man's work. She could do it a damn sight better than most men, she told him.

He asked her if she'd be down at the cross that night with the others, and she said yes she would. They were shy of each other at first, but they ended up staying talking for hours after everyone else had left, until it was dark.

I asked Gran what they talked about but she couldn't really remember. 'Probably silly nonsense,' she said. 'Probably we didn't even make sense.'

Then he walked her home and kissed her on the cheek.

She told her mother she'd been helping over at the neighbours'. 'Haven't we enough to be getting on with here,' was her mother's weary response.

Every evening after that they'd meet. They took to swimming in the lake together. Felim was a much better swimmer than she was. He was like a fish in the water, she said. He could hold his breath for ages. It'd frighten her sometimes he'd stay under that long. But she got used to it. She started to think he might even be able to breathe under there. Everyone knew that he was the best swimmer in the county. Ever since he was little. She'd stand very still waiting for him to surface, her limbs starting to go wobbly with the cold, and he'd bubble out of the water right behind her, or he'd nibble at the calf of her leg, or pull her under with him sometimes.

She couldn't remember rightly how long it was before she realised she was going to have a baby. She was just sixteen. She didn't say a word to anyone, and she stopped going down to see Felim, though he went on waiting for her every night on the lane.

She couldn't hide the bump for long. As soon as they found out, she was sent to her aunt's in the next county over. That was the only time her father ever belted her, right across the face with his bare hand. He didn't say a single word to her after that. And her mother could barely look at her. Still, it was better they sent her to her aunt's than to one of those unmarried mothers' homes she might never have come out of.

Her Aunt Bridie was a cleaner up at one of the Big Houses. She was away most of the time, which suited Gran. She was left to keep her house. She'd do the washing, scrub the floors, bake bread, make sure her uncle's dinner was on the table at six each evening. Right up until she gave birth. Bridie was firm but kind. She made sure she was well fed, and she gave her her own settle by the fire in the kitchen. And Uncle Frank kept himself to himself, which was no bad thing in those times. He had nothing kind to say to her, but nor did he treat her badly. Their own children were away abroad and knew nothing about what was going on.

The baby girl was born in summer. Gran hadn't really thought what would happen after that, and her aunt hadn't said a word about it. She fell in love with that baby straight away. She wasn't like some mothers who couldn't bear the sight of this squawking thing that had caused them so much pain. Hers was a quiet wee thing. Which was a good thing, she thought, otherwise it'd have driven her aunt and uncle to despair. Weeks went by, and she grew less and less concerned. She thought her aunt and uncle might just keep her and the child on indefinitely. Or she could take her home and all would be forgiven once they saw that she was the most beautiful child anyone ever set eyes on. She wrote letters to her mother, telling her all about her new baby. How perfect she was, how good-natured, how much she resembled her grandmother. She'd walk for miles to the nearest post office to send the letters. But she never heard anything back.

She was out in the farm collecting eggs when her uncle took the baby. Bridie wouldn't tell her where, only that it would be safe and happy, and in God's hands. Gran carried on at Bridie's for another while – she didn't remember how long, weeks, maybe months even. She was no good to her parents in the state she was in. In any case, she wouldn't leave the house, wouldn't set foot outside the front door. Not since they'd taken Celia away.

Maybe if she had she might have been able to get her back.

They'd brought Celia to the industrial school in town. The infirmary was run by a young nun called Mother Michael. Years later Gran saw the room where she'd been nursed, since turned into a classroom. There was a poster on the wall that said 'The family who prays together stays together'. Mother Michael pointed to where all the cots used to be. She told her how she used to feed all the babies with mashed egg and potatoes from the same spoon, their mouths open like little scaldíns. She remembered little Celie always being hungrier than the rest of them. She told her how some of the older orphans would dote on the babies, look after them like they were their own. It was that same nun had sent the photograph of Celia to Gran years later, telling her she was happily 'placed' with a family in England.

Mam and Dad were over at the neighbours' for drinks. I chose the bottle from the drinks cabinet that had been there so long no one would notice it missing. The rim was sticky. And it was sweet, that peach schnapps. I took the bottle and a glass to my room, swigging the first glass fairly quickly, and the second. By the third my head was like lead, but feathery with it. I could see particles move round the room – particles of the *room* move round the room, like jigsaw pieces. Clearly I could see them, like the jagged little lights that fall in front of your eyes sometimes. My mouth tasted of purple clover. I sucked the air in through pouted lips to savour the cold on the sweet, moist fleshiness of my tongue. I was fearless with love, red-blooded. Blood throbbing in my ears. I peered out into the dark, longing to see Leon peer back in at me. I laughed at my own reflection, my face up close to the mirror. And I danced, bouncing off the walls.

I kissed the window pane.

Then I felt the dampness on my chest. I put my hand to my face: it was slippery with tears, and sticky around the corners of my mouth. My nose was streaming. Flopping down on the bed, I sobbed and sobbed until my head hurt. I could barely see I cried so much. This was just what I'd been after. I knew where I was with this.

'Dearest Leon,' I wrote,

I'm sorry about that night at the concert. I didn't mean it. I swear I didn't. But why did you lie to me? I wouldn't have minded if you'd told me the truth. I thought you cared about me, and now you're ignoring me. Have I done something wrong? It hurts so much not to see you, not to talk to you. You should have told me. You did see me on Christmas Day, didn't you? What am I supposed to do? Do you hate me? I love you. I don't mind telling you. I love you, I love you, I love you, and you have to trust me. If you can't trust me then we have nothing. I'm not just some stupid girl. I don't want you to think that. I know what I want. And you can't treat me like I don't exist. Because I do. And I'll always love you. So you better get used to the idea. And please don't think I'm a stupid girl, because I'm not. I can't imagine how difficult things must have been for you, but I'm here if you need me. I want to give myself to you. I want you to have me. I'm all yours. Surely you would have had to tell me some day, or I would have found out somehow? Or was this just some stupid fling? We were just supposed to get off with each

other a couple of times and that was it? I don't understand.
Please write. I beg you.

Love for ever
Lani

I woke in the morning to find vomit on my duvet and down the side of the bed. I cleaned up as much as I could, but I'm sure Mam would have smelled it if she'd come in. If she did she never said anything.

The sound of the knife in her skin. The Child of Prague in the window. The neighbours' light going on. His heavy eyelids drooping again. A bubble of spit at the corner of her mouth. His father tucking him in, saying *It's all right now, son, it's only a bad dream.* That dark house. The pretty blonde lady sleeping in bed. His whole body shaking. Her body on the floor, slumped on her front, like she was sunbathing or sleeping. Avoiding making eye contact with the dead woman. Blood on the bedclothes and on the carpet. Him downstairs preparing, before the steps, before the lights went out, before his son slept. Like foxes out in the dark. Her screeching. The little boy sleeping. And the ambulance men taking her away. His face all lit up with hate. The boy on the landing being hushed into a spare bedroom. The puncturing. His father saying *He never is.* The way the guards must have crouched down by the body, crossed themselves. Their silence. Leon boiling potatoes for his father. His sweet little face. And her eyes set on something in the distance. His quiet steps as he climbed the stairs to his son's room.

CR

I lay out in the snow on New Year's Eve until the cold had seeped into me, until I had become tiny with the cold, brittle-boned. I couldn't think what else to do. Mar and I hadn't spoken since that last day before the holidays, and Mam and Dad wouldn't let me go out. There was no way, they said – not until they were sure they could trust me again. I carried on like someone possessed, told them they were evil, that every other girl in my year would be out that night, that I was old enough to do what I liked. But there was nothing I could do.

I lay under the swing, flat on my back, my arms and legs out like a starfish, and waited for the night to take hold of me. It was like I was a glass paperweight. No, a cut diamond – all sharp edges – gazing up at the cloudless sky. No one came. No one came to find me. Twelve o'clock came and went and I was all alone.

All the rest of the holiday I sat in my room staring at

the walls. Or watched telly in the front room. I felt like I was outside looking in, at this family playing happy families, living on the outskirts of the universe – my father lighting big fires in the evenings, my mother looking younger, sweeter than I ever remembered her. She and Gran taking turns with the one pack of cards, playing endless games of Patience. When Mam wasn't playing that she was knitting – a tiny white cardigan, which I was sure would be too small for the baby. It was doll-sized. She had beautiful pearly white buttons for it. I have this image of her still, her face bathed in the light from the fire, her feet stretched out in front of her, crossed at the ankles, and the movement of her wrists, plain and purl stitching that little cardigan, the knitting needles clicking.

Josie, 15

Margaret is my favourite friend, even though she doesn't think she is. She is the best in the class and she helps me when I don't know something. She tried to kill herself once. I might try to do it but Miss Dolan says if you take your own life you burn in hell for eternity. She also says never to point a knife at anyone because it's bad luck, and that her brother saw a leprechaun once, and that she nearly died but she prayed very hard to Jesus and he saved her. I try to imagine what it would be like to be burning for ever, with the devil standing over you, poking you with his fork. Then I have awful nightmares and wake up all covered in sweat. Margaret says there is no such thing as hell, and anyway we'd be better off there. She doesn't want me to kill myself, though. She says I should work hard at my school work and then get a job outside of here.

I've only been in the town once. That was on the

way to visit the bishop. Mother Andrew gave me money and told me to go into the shop and buy a nice cake for the bishop. I didn't know what to do. The shop-keeper looked at me like I was a leper. 'Well, are you wanting to buy something or what?' she said. Mother Andrew had to come in after me and do it for me. 'Thank you, Sister,' the shopkeeper said to her, smiling. She should have said 'Mother'. Later, when no one was looking, Mother got me by the ear and twisted it until I couldn't feel it anymore.

I didn't know what I was supposed to do at the bishop's house, until I realised that I was there to help clean. He was having special visitors from Dublin. Not the Pope, but somebody almost as important.

I don't know what I want to be when I grow up like Margaret. I can't say I want to be a nurse like her because she says I am copying her. I don't want to be a shopkeeper. Maybe I will work as a cleaner at the bishop's house. He was nice to me.

I took to eating only Rich Tea biscuits – and drinking lots of tea, lots of milky tea. My variation on a bread-and-water diet. It helped with the emptiness in my head somehow, to feel my stomach empty too. I liked the black spells when I stood up too quickly. And I smoked as many cigarettes as I could cadge or steal at school. They made my head go like a hive full of bees. Mam fussed over me at mealtimes – poor Mam must have been beside herself – but I made such a scene every time she tried to make me eat that she soon learned to just let me be. Mar and I had hardly said two words to each other, except when we were forced to in class, and it was easier to pretend everything was normal than to have the teachers on our backs. Then one morning she arrived into school in a terrible state. We went to the cloakroom at break time that morning, like we used to.

'Eoin rang me last night,' she sobbed. 'He said he had

too much study to do for the exams and we wouldn't be able to see each other for ages, so we might as well break up. He said he didn't want to but what could we do.'

I put my arm around her, but could think of nothing to say. She was having one of those crying fits where it's hard to breathe and words come out all wonky.

'He said he loved me,' she wailed. 'The fucking bastard! He only said that so he could get into my knickers. And now I think I might be up the duff.'

'What do you mean?'

'What do you mean what do I mean?'

'God, Mar, weren't you using protection?'

'Yeah, but I don't think it worked. I feel kind of weird.'

She did look a little pale.

'Don't worry. We'll buy a pregnancy test at the weekend. Then you'll see. I'm sure you're not.'

'I'm sorry I've been such a bitch, Lani. And I'm sorry about you and Leon.'

'How do you mean?'

'Eoin told me.'

'Eoin told you what?'

'That you'd broken up.'

Then *I* felt sick. Really sick.

'That's a lie,' I said, my voice jarring in my throat.

'He's a freak anyway. Don't worry. You can do better than him. He's not even *that* good-looking.'

'What the hell's that got to do with anything?'

'Everyone knows about him, Lani. About his father.'

I really lost it then.

'Just shut up, Mar. Shut up, you *stupid fucking* BITCH.' I spat at her — right between the eyes. I hadn't spat since I was a kid. It felt good, getting that little ball of anger out of me. I watched it slowly slither down either side of the bridge of her nose.

She went all still, her arms stretched out as if she wanted her hands as far away from herself as possible. She pulled a sleeve down and wiped it away quickly. 'I think I'm going to be sick,' she said. Then she started to scream: 'You fucking deserve him, you *weirdo freaking creep*! You're like the Mr and Mrs Freak of Freaksville, Tennessee.'

I remember marvelling at her way with words, even in a situation such as this — one that would leave most speechless. It wasn't long before one of the teachers came to find out what all the noise was, and hauled us off to the headmistress's office.

We told her we'd been just messing. 'She tickled me is all, Miss,' Mar said, 'and I screamed. I didn't mean to.'

'I don't know what's happened to you, Miss Halpern. You used to be such a nice girl. Your grades are going down, and I'm sick of seeing you in this office. I don't want to see you in here again. And as for you, Miss Devine, I thought you'd know better. Get out of my sight, the pair of you.'

I hoped Mar *was* pregnant and would have to leave school and live in a caravan in the woods, all alone, and be disowned by all her family and friends, and have to go on the dole, and spend her days hand-washing cloth nappies. Then she'd wish she'd been nicer to me.

I knelt at Hermione's grave that evening and cried. A thick fog blanketed the countryside. I could barely see an arm's length in front of me. Leon never showed. I did have the feeling I was being watched though. Then it wouldn't be the last time I'd feel that way. I liked it. He could watch me break my heart over him if that's what he wanted. I was worn out with it. I stayed there until the cold had seeped right into me, the fog had made its way into my clothes.

Dinner was on the table when I got home, Mam and Dad both ready to tell me off for being late until they saw the state I was in. I went straight to my room without uttering a word. Mam followed.

'What's the matter, love?'

'Nothing. I just want to be on my own.'

She sat down on the bed beside me, right up close, put her hand on my knee.

'Is it the baby? Is it because you had to move out of your room? Because you didn't want to move out of your room? Because you don't have to, love, you know. You don't have to do anything you don't want to. We'll think of something else.'

'No. Just leave me alone, will you?'

'What's gotten *in*to you, Lani? Is this about Blue?'

I was crying again. 'Just leave me alone.'

'You really should eat something, you know, love. I'll leave something out for you.'

She shut the door gently behind her, not clicking the latch so it creaked open again moments later. I stood up and slammed it shut. I didn't want to be able to hear her and Dad murmuring about me over dinner, and I didn't want to have to smell the stinking cabbage smell of food.

❧

Dear Leon,

What have I done to deserve this? Why are you telling everyone else but me that you've dumped me? I need you so much. Don't you understand? I'm terrified that you think that I didn't want to be with you. I desperately did. I wanted to give myself to you, but it never seemed like the right time.

Is there anything I can do to make you change your mind? I'm sure that you can't have been lying to me that whole time. I know I hurt you. But you hurt me too. Please, <u>please</u> tell me what I can do to make it up to you.

Love,
Lani

He was in the town one Saturday a couple of weeks later. In the hardware section of Tesco. It gave me an awful fright. I had to get the keys from Mam and run out to the car before he saw me. I hadn't washed my hair in days. It was stuck to my head with grease, all frizzy with split ends. My skin had gone all red and flaky – from not eating properly, I suppose. He couldn't see me like that. That wasn't supposed to be how it went.

He came out of the supermarket with a girl walking behind him who I'd not seen before – about his age, with long straight caramel-coloured hair. It was hard to tell if she was pretty from where I was.

I sank down into the back seat of the car and watched them walk across the car park towards the same car he'd been driving that time I'd seen him at Christmas. They weren't holding hands or anything like that. He walked faster than her, even with the trolley. She had to trot to keep up.

I didn't even notice Mam knocking on the driver's seat window for me to let her in.

'Would you ever help me with this shopping, Lani? What use are you to me sitting back there?'

Mam grabbed my arm as I lifted a bag into the boot.

'What's the matter with you, Lani? You're shaking like a leaf. Right, that's it, I'm making an appointment with the doctor as soon as we get home. I'm not having you carry on like this anymore.'

I said nothing, though I knew I wasn't going to see a doctor. She couldn't make me. I felt cold as anything. I saw Leon's car drive off, with that girl in the passenger seat.

When we got home Mam unpacked vitamins, cod-liver oil capsules, garlic pills, evening primrose oil and St John's Wort.

'These are for you, Lani. And I'm going to call the doctor right now.'

'If you do I won't eat.'

'You're hardly eating anyway.'

I called her a bitch and ran outside, slamming the back door behind me, Mam shouting 'What did you say? Get back in here, young lady.'

I turned up Molly's lane before reaching the graveyard. I knew they wouldn't think to look for me up there. I'd said often enough I was terrified of Molly's dog. Which I was. I was hoping for a gruesome attack, something that would leave its mark on me. Something cathartic. My blood tingled imagining its teeth sinking into my flesh.

'She hates me. I hate her. She hates me. I hate her,' I

chanted in my head. 'I'll show them. I'll make them see. I'll show them . . .'

The land on either side felt like it was closing in on me. There were rivers of rainbow oil on the stagnant water in the ditches. Molly was in the yard with a bucket of seed, feeding the few chickens she had fenced in at the front of the house. She was almost bent double with arthritis. The skin on her arms and face was dark with sun and dirt, and her thin white hair was like fine doll's hair. She had on a blue nylon dress, bright green socks over sagging brown nylon tights, and black laced boots. She looked up and eyed me suspiciously. She said something but I couldn't hear. I was too far away yet to make out her words. I pretended not to see her, pretended she was invisible. She carried on with what she was doing and ignored me. The dog – a fierce-looking Alsatian tied to the inside of the gate – started to bark, straining at the end of its leash. I turned suddenly, and walked as fast as I could back to the main road before she let him loose on me. That's what she was supposed to do – set the dog on me. That's what people said she did. Sometimes she even wielded a kitchen knife, I'd heard, and would sharpen it as people walked past. That's how crazy she was. And she spoke in words that made no sense. Chicken and dog words. My heart was racing. I pulled myself back just long enough for a car to whizz past before I crossed over to the cemetery. There were two people walking down the middle path, hand in hand. I nodded at them as they looked over. They nodded back. The dog was still barking.

No sign of my parents out looking for me. Or Leon. I sat down in the same spot under the cross, and waited for them to come and find me. I watched the lights come on in the house across the way, and the watery sunlight melting into the hills that turned the shale I was sitting on to a deep greyish-purple, and still there was no sign of them. There was nothing for it but to go home and wait in the back garden until someone showed up.

It was still just bright enough outside that I could make my way to the swing at the back of the house without stumbling and making noise. It was darker under there than anywhere else in the garden. The only sound was the fizzing river, and the squeaking of the branches above as I swung over and back, over and back, deeper into the night, over the river, higher and higher. The cold swam through me. The air whistled around my empty belly. I closed my eyes, put my head back and my feet in the air, so that I was lying flat and could no longer tell where I was – near to the ground or tipping the branches. Then the only sound was the whooshing in my ears. I couldn't stop, though I felt sick. Still they didn't come for me. Finally I pulled myself back up and wound the ropes around each other, looking up into the branches, until it looked like the tree was moving while I sat perfectly still. I felt hands on my shoulders and screamed, something I hadn't done since I was a child. Then a face went whirling past in the darkness with the tree, and disappeared. 'It's only me,' it said.

I was sobbing, choking on my tears, when Mam and Dad found me and unwound the ropes from above my head.

'Are you okay, pet? What's happened?'

'Nothing. I got a fright – that's all.'

'What was that?' Dad asked, peering through to the field. 'Jesus, there's somebody there.'

Mam clung to me, while Dad made his way to the gate and shouted, 'Go on. If I catch you around here again I'll call the guards. Go on.'

'It was probably just a fox or something,' Mam said, wiping away the tears from my face.

'That was no fox.'

Their faces were blue from the porch light.

'Get into that house now, the pair of you.'

Mam held me by the wrist, afraid to let me go, afraid I'd be pulled out to the river man. Dad stood at the back door, chest puffed out, peering after whoever it was had dared set foot near our home in the night.

'You see what I told you. It's not safe to be gallivanting out there on your own at night,' Mam said, sitting me down at the dining room table then automatically flicking the switch on the kettle.

'I've a good mind to call the guards,' Dad said as he stepped into the room, visibly shaken.

'Please don't, Daddy,' I said. 'It was nothing.'

'Well, I don't care. That's it now, Lani. No more wandering off on your own. Do you hear me?'

'Yes, Daddy.'

I was sure my eyes were like two beacons. I kept them lowered so neither of them would see.

That night I dreamt that I was over at the neighbours' with Blue. We followed her trail back over the front lawn, around the side of the house and down to the back garden. When I looked up at the house there were hundreds of Friesian cows, all gawping at us, ready to stampede. I was terrified. Blue barked and barked at them. Her barks made no sound. Somehow we managed to reach the back door. Inside the house was flooded, all the furniture gone, or what remained broken and floating on the water. Sunlight streamed in the windows. The cows were there too. I fell to the ground or sank, I'm not sure, and some boy, whose face I couldn't see, stretched my arms up above my head and tickled me. I was helpless to do anything. I couldn't move from the floor. My clothes were soaking wet. The boy smiled. The cows looked on, moving slowly towards me. The tickling was unbearable. I woke with the pain of it, sweating.

Elaine, 16

I was twelve when I came here first. Most of the girls were younger, so I suppose that made me a bit different. They took me out of school when I was thirteen, for biting one of the townies. She was going on at one of the little ones, 'Lady Muck, Lady Muck, with your scabby, dirty head. Give us a slurp of that cocoa,' and she knocked the cup out of her hand and scalded her knees. I bit her on the ear and had the shite beaten out of me, and told I'd be off to a reformatory the next time I carried on like that. They needed me in the convent anyway. I'm good with my hands. And they like to keep a close eye on me.

I used to talk to Angela but her head's up her arse. She thinks she's the chosen one because Mother Assumpta wants to put her hands in her drawers. Who is she trying to cod?

They said I was too big for my boots when I got here

first, and they'd have to put manners on me. Mother Margaret put me in a bath with three other girls and stood watching me, ordering me to scrub behind them filthy ears of mine, and down between my legs. And then I was made wear pants made out of flour sacks. And hobnail boots. I'm used to them now. The boots are good for clobbering the younger ones when they're bold.

I am one of four children. Maisie and me, and the other two – a boy and a girl, if I remember rightly – who died before I was born. And then my mother died when I was five. I don't remember her at all. I saw some pictures, but that was a long time ago. Sometimes when I catch sight of myself in a mirror I think I might look a bit like her. My father looked after the three of us. Maisie, the older one, did most of the cooking and cleaning, though Daddy used to like to make us boiled eggs and soldiers on Sundays.

One of my favourite things was going down with him to the sucking calves, and them slobbering all over my fingers with their big pink tongues.

Daddy got very sick with TB and couldn't look after us properly anymore, and Maisie couldn't cope. He died when I was fourteen and a half. I wasn't allowed go to the funeral. They said I would be too upset. My sister Maisie went though. She was working as a cleaner up at St Colum's College. She's in one of them Magdalene homes now.

There were primroses along the bank of the river at the back of the house, wood sorrel close to the school. It was Leon's last few months before exams. After that he'd be gone from the place for good. I wouldn't get to watch his lengthening shadow on the road. I thought about starving myself into oblivion, but I couldn't as long as there was still a chance. I couldn't leave. In bed early every night, I'd turn off the light and replay the same fantasy. It went like this: *My darling Lani, I have made such a terrible mistake. We must be together,* etcetera, etcetera. Cut to: meeting under big trees, green light filtering through the leaves: *Lani, can you ever forgive me?* Pan to my face, radiant with love and tenderness, and to his eyes, welling with tears of such gratitude. Then the kiss, better than anything ever in the world before this. And his arms around me for all eternity.

Nothing beyond that point: though sometimes I could drag it out for a long time, I could never go beyond. I either rolled over and went to sleep with a smile on my face or broke down and wept. More and more frequently I'd get up and go to the kitchen late at night and eat. I was sick of Rich Tea biscuits. And I'd fainted in class from the hunger one day, which was mortifying. I didn't want that happening again, though it was nice that Mar was the first one I saw crouching down beside me when I came to, looking all concerned.

I'd melt cooking chocolate in a glass bowl over boiling water and dip bananas into it – not just one, but several at a time, and scoff them almost without taking a breath. Then I'd go outside and smoke two or three cigarettes. That was the time to eat – late at night when no one could see, no one could watch me, so it didn't count, it wasn't real.

I was sneaking into Gran's room whenever I could too, to stare at that picture of Celia when she was young, and that picture of Gran when she was the age I was then. Trying to imagine what it must have been like for her, never seeing Felim again.

It's a wonder I wasn't killed that day, I cycled so fast. I didn't even get off the bike for the hills, as I usually would. The sweat was pouring off me by the time I got out to Crogher. I felt dizzy, like I'd been swimming in cold water for too long. I knew where his house was. I'd seen the address in the phone book. It was at the end of a row of semi-detached houses painted in pinks and beiges and creams, with clashing primaries on the window shutters and the doors, all clean and neatly ordered, with privet hedges either side, and tiny, perfectly manicured lawns. Pansy beds in the garden to the right of his, roses in the other. No Child of Prague in the window. Only two garden gnomes on the lawn. Along the side of the garden was a path leading to an old derelict farmhouse behind. I put my bike in the ditch and walked down to the old house. I didn't even try to hide myself. His father could kill me, for all I cared.

The front door was broken off its hinges, hanging by a

last nail from the door frame. A big sturdy wooden door, with double-bolted latches. The darkness inside smelled of lighter fuel and something else which I couldn't quite make out. I think it must have been the damp horsehair spewing from the old mattresses upstairs. There were the remnants of a campfire in the middle of what would have been the kitchen floor. The floor was bare cement, with bits of dirty red lino in places, and old brown and green bottles of animal medicine, and ketchup and rat poison strewn about the place. There were layers of wallpaper on some sections of the wall, peeling back generations of roses, brocade; other bits of wall were bare plaster and had been daubed with paint, most of it indecipherable. 'Fuck the world' it said on one section in large red letters.

Upstairs that smell got more potent. The old metal-framed bedsteads with their striped mattresses were damp, fetid. Rats' nests. The windows were deeply set. From the biggest bedroom I could see right into Leon's house. Scratched into the sill was my name, clear as anything.

There was some movement on the stairs. I looked for somewhere to hide, then thought better of it. Leon appeared at the door.

'Lani, what are you doing here?' He didn't even look surprised to see me. He looked upset, more than anything.

'I wanted to see you,' I said. 'You've not been responding to my letters.'

'I'm going away soon. I'll be finished school and then I'll be going away. To university, hopefully.'

'What's that got to do with anything?'

'Well, there's no point in us . . . Is there? I'll be gone.'

'But I could come with you.'

'No, you couldn't,' he said, and that was that. He seemed certain. 'Now you better go. I don't want my father finding you here.'

'But that was you in my garden the other night . . .'

'I just wanted to see you before I went,' he said.

'Is it because of that girl?'

'What girl?'

'That one I saw you in town with.'

'There's no one else,' he said, and somehow I believed him.

I thought if I could just get him to put his arms around me then everything would be okay. Maybe I could trick him, feign sickness . . .

'I'm really sorry,' he said, but he didn't come any nearer. He kept his eyes fixed on some point on the floor beyond me, as if he was afraid to look at me for shame. I could feel my insides collapse – first my heart, then my lungs, then my stomach. I couldn't breathe. I wanted to be sick. I put my hand out for something to touch.

'Could you not come with me? Back home?' I pleaded, knowing as I said it that it would sound stupid.

He shifted from where he stood. 'No,' he said. 'I can't.' Like that. Very definite. That was all. Then he turned his back on me and walked out.

'Please,' I shouted, louder than I'd meant.

It was like I'd been kicked in the guts. I bent over, my head swimming, then crumpled to the floor.

He'd come back.

I made circles in the dust with my hands as the tears recklessly flowed.

He would come. He wouldn't leave me like that.

I don't know how long I stayed there waiting. An hour maybe.

I managed to get home, though I could barely see I was crying so much.

'What in God's name happened to you?' Gran asked when she saw the state I was in.

I tried to rub the dirt from my hands onto my jeans. 'Nothing, Gran,' I said, 'I just had a fight with Mar.'

Gran took a sherry bottle from behind her armchair and told me get two glasses. Sherry had always been her favourite tipple, she said, even as a youngster. That's what she'd been drinking the night she met my grandfather, Lazy Bones. She was playing poker in an upstairs room in a bar. She was cleaning them out. He walked her home, told her a public house was no place for a lady like her, and they were married a year after. She thought she'd die an old spinster but there she was with a chance of making a go of things. And then a son joining the priesthood. And a daughter happily married . . .

'But what about Felim, Gran? Weren't you still in love with him?'

'Of course I was. But what could I do? We couldn't get married. We were too young. And his family had nothing. As far as he was concerned I was that girl who'd left him waiting, night after night – for nigh on a year, someone told me he waited. It would have been better if it had stayed that way, but someone told him about Celia. I still don't know who it was. He never would have forgiven me for that anyway. He went and got married, to some local girl, and that was that.'

Patsy, 6

My brother says I have to be good for the nuns. There isn't enough food at home and I'm a good girl, my mammy said I was, she said I was a good girl and I was eating her out of house and home. I was crying but I promised her I wouldn't but she promised me and she was crying. My brother took me on his bike. I can ride a bike. He taught me but he said it was too long. We went into the ditch because he said I was too heavy and I got stings on my legs I still have them they hurt. The nun gave me stings on my legs with her stick for not being a good girl even though I was. I don't like my nuniform. It bites me under my arms. If I am a good girl for three days my brother will come and get me back I won't eat everything only my fair share because I eat less than the baby here only old potato and water that doesn't taste like anything and my mammy knows how to make it. I am a good girl and do the ABC at the big school that I learn at the little school at home. I do numbers as well and I can count 1 2 3 4 5 6 7 8 9 10 Miss Dolan told me that I learn it with orange pieces but the oarfin girls weren't allowed to eat it only the good girls from outside the school they go home to their mammies because they are good and they don't wear nuniforms the same as me.

It was around Easter time, I remember. I hated Easter. Ash Wednesday especially. All the girls at school walking around with big grey smudges on their foreheads. And having to kiss the feet of Jesus on the cross, and the priest wiping away your spit with a handkerchief before the next girl. It felt rude, kissing that naked man's feet. Especially in front of everyone else. Even if it was only a statue.

Mam was saying that she remembered all the little orphan girls getting a giant Easter egg delivered to the school.

'D'you know, I used to be kind of envious of them,' she said. 'They'd get this big Easter egg every year, delivered to the school gates, and our eyes'd be popping out of our heads. All we got were boiled eggs at Easter. They weren't allowed to have those Easter eggs though. The nuns confiscated them. But sure I didn't realise that at the time. I remember Mammy giving me food to bring in to them – and me being embarrassed in front of the other girls, and the teacher giving me dirty looks. Sometimes I didn't even give it to them. I gave it to my friends instead.'

'You never told me that,' Gran said. 'It was rhubarb from our garden.'

Mam had been a day girl at the convent school in town years after the fire. She remembered the little orphans in their calico dresses at the back of the class, always quiet and smelling of disinfectant. And their little hands red raw. She remembered one of them weeing herself in class one day and her being beaten black and blue for it. No one would talk to them. They weren't allowed.

'We thought it was normal,' Mam said. 'Sure we didn't know any different.'

Most of those girls were in England now. One had worked up at the boys' school as a cleaner for years. She lived in the small house by the school gates. Maisie, they called her. I knew her to see about the town. She'd be wearing a wig sat on her head like a hat, and layers and layers of dirty clothes. The stink off her was so bad you'd have to cross the road if you saw her coming.

Mam and I walked past the old convent school one Saturday afternoon when we were in getting some groceries. We stopped in front of the iron gates that lead into the court-yard.

'Your grandmother walked past this place every day for two years after she was married.'

'I didn't know.'

'No, I don't think she ever told anyone before. Sure how could she, with Father . . . He was so good to her . . .'

It turned out Gran had been there the morning after the fire. They'd said the girls did so much polishing it had gone up like a box of matches. She could remember the stench in the town afterwards. She still got that smell sometimes. It was hard to think that those little girls could smell so awful.

She'd got herself a job as a cleaner at the surgical hospital in town, across the road from the orphanage, after she'd pleaded with her uncle to tell her where they'd taken Celia. On her lunch breaks she'd go across and peer into the yard, where the girls were out playing. You'd hardly know there were children in there, it was so quiet.

People must have thought she was queer, always going over there. But no one ever said anything. And she never let on that she'd had a baby. Not even to her closest friend.

How she was able to go there, day after day, and see the little girls from the convent, I don't know. How she could bear to see the blacked-up, barred windows.

After the fire, she was broken. But there was no way she could let on. She had to keep it all inside her. My grandfather was all she had left in the world.

She watched the coffins being carried out – eight of them for thirty-five girls – thinking Celia was in one of them. There was a mass in the convent, but she didn't go. It was for the official people of the town only. It would have looked strange for her to be there. She followed the cortege up to the graveyard though. She watched them lower the coffins into the ground. She heard the priest call them little angels.

And later she went back to the convent and she walked up to the door. One of the nuns peered from behind a grille. She told her she would have to come back another time, but Gran went hysterical on her. The nun opened the door and stood facing away from her. She wasn't allowed even to look outside. She wouldn't even make eye contact with her, Gran said.

Gran explained to her about Celia.

She was told that no one under the age of two had been killed in the fire, and the likelihood was that that particular child had been adopted. She wouldn't tell her any more than that.

The hoops were still left up against the wall inside in the courtyard, where the little girls had been playing with them just the day before.

Catherine, 10

My mammy didn't want me to come here. She didn't have a pension but. That's what you need when you're old and your husband died and left you with seven children. My auntie and uncle took me. They used to be my favourites until they did that. I thought they were going to keep me for themselves. They probably would have, except I started to do things my auntie didn't like. I didn't like it either. Except when my uncle gave me a hula hoop, and a doll with a porcelain head.

All the girls here sleep in beds very close together. Sometimes I try to get into bed with Sheila and she whispers very loud at me to 'Get out, get out.' She is more scared than me. I don't care.

We have hula hoops. We're supposed to share. We play with them in the yard. I can do it around my neck and belly. No one else can. It's because I got to practise before I came. My uncle counted how many times I could do it without stopping.

We drink chestnut water in the summer. It's our special treat. We make it out of leaves and sugar in the field at the back of the convent. You have to crush the leaves down until there is the chestnut juice, which is green, and then you add the sugar and some water. Sometimes I get the sugar. I am supposed to be putting it in my cocoa and I put it into my hand under the table instead. And then I keep it in my pocket until we go outside. My pocket gets sticky but I don't care. Chestnut water is nicer than cocoa. Cocoa has things wriggling in it. And then they put the boiling water in on top of them and they're dead.

My auntie is nicer to me now. She brings me sweets sometimes. But when she brings them the nuns take them off me. I just want one. The nuns will get very fat if they eat all our sweets all the time. Mother Assumpta says if I'm a good girl she will get me some.

❧

My grandfather had been in with friends, in their kitchen playing penny poker, the night of the fire. There was some commotion outside on the street. A few of them went out to see what it was, and saw the smoke billowing from the convent, and its doors still firmly closed.

He went over, shouting for someone to come and open the door. Finally, after several of the men had tried to break through with axes and pokers and whatever they could lay their hands on, they were let into the courtyard.

There were men shouting, 'Get them out!' and car horns going off, and people running about in all directions, not knowing what to do. No one knew the layout of the place. And it was dark, and there was a lot of smoke.

He ran up the fire escape, but the door at the top was locked. He tried to boot it open but he couldn't. The next time he tried to go up with the keys the smoke was too thick. Some of the other men were trying to put the fire out in the laundry, but it was getting worse.

Men were passing out.

The children were screaming that they were burning.

Ladders had been brought, but they weren't long enough and the soldiers at the top of them were trying to encourage some of the girls to jump.

My grandfather had seen those little girls at the windows. He'd heard them praying and crying, and the one girl with the soles of her shoes on fire . . . A friend who was there with him that night said one of the children that was persuaded to jump slipped through a man's arms right in front of him, crushing her legs.

He helped some of the older girls take the young ones to safety. The babies from the infirmary.

The worst of it was that had the men not been there so soon after the fire started, the nuns might have let the little girls out. It was from their eyes they were protecting them. The girls were made to get down on their knees and say decades of the rosary rather than escape outdoors and run the risk of being seen in their nighties.

Mam took it very easy, as advised, except for the odd trip into town to buy provisions – nappies, baby-gros, Sudocrem. Even Dad, who'd usually wait in the car with the key in the ignition while Mam and I shopped, was keen to tag along on those little excursions.

I had exams coming up and I had a lot of cramming to do before then. As hard as I tried, though, I'd still end up staring out the window, recalling things Leon had said to me, or ways he'd looked at me, and my chest would feel like it was filling up with helium.

Mostly I wouldn't allow myself to think about him, but every now and again, when no one else was around – especially in bed at night – I'd try to let the whole of the past few months go, and imagine that we were about to start again. That it was only the beginning. He would take me away with him, wherever he was going. He wouldn't leave without me. He was just putting things right at home, thinking of ways that we could be together.

Mam gave birth to a little girl on 10 May. Dad phoned us with the news sometime after four in the afternoon. A beautiful little girl, he said. Seven pound five ounces. It was the same kind of feeling I had when I thought about Leon: that swelling in my chest, like a balloon being pumped up inside of me. A beautiful little girl, I repeated to myself, as I ran outside to Gran to tell her.

Mam was in one of those same wards she'd been in when I was born, with the windows that opened out onto the veranda and down to a perfect lawn. The fallen petals of the cherry blossoms made little pink whirlpools on the grass. She was sitting up in bed, wearing a white cotton nightgown buttoned low at the front so you could see the blue veins on her breasts. Her bed was right by the window, the sun streaming in on her. I wanted to pull the curtain around the bed, to shield her from all the other women in the room. She looked older than they did, more tired. There were little streaks of grey tucked behind her ears.

The baby was in a glass cot beside her. Dad held on to Gran as I approached. I was embarrassed. She was so tiny it was embarrassing. And everyone looking at me to see what I'd do.

'Say hello to your big sister,' Mam was cooing.

The baby's nails were transparent. She had fair hair, like mine, and she had on a little white baby-gro and the wee white cardigan Mam had knitted for her. Her head was turned to the side, her little tongue curling out of her mouth. Her cheeks all pink and chapped. Tiny little nostrils. Mam smiled so sweetly when I turned to look at her.

I handed her the sprig of purple heather I'd been holding since we left the house.

'This is for you, Mam. And the baby.'

'Thank you, love,' she said, and took my hand. I squeezed hers as tightly as I could without hurting her, and didn't let go as Gran kissed her and cooed at the baby.

'She looks like an Erica, doesn't she, Dad? What do you think?' Mam smiled.

'Yes, after the heather – *Erica cinerea*. She does indeed.'

And she did, with her pinched little nose, and her velvety eyes that opened just as Gran leaned over to look at her.

I called Mar that night to tell her. She took ages to come to the phone.

'Listen, Mar, I'm really sorry about spitting on you.'

She didn't say anything.

'Mar, are you there? Mar?' I could hear her breathing.

'Forget it, okay,' she said.

'I didn't mean to.'

'Yeah, I know, it just came out!'

I could hear her smiling then.

'You'll be pleased to hear I wasn't pregnant after all.'

'Yeah, well, I guessed as much. Would have noticed the bump. I told you you wouldn't be anyway.'

She came over to see Erica the following week.

'God, would you look at how tiny she is!'

'Wait till you smell her. It's like . . . so sweet . . . I can't explain.'

Mam held Erica's little baby head out to us and we both breathed in the soft smell of newborn, and had her squeeze our fingers with her tiny little fist.

Things were strange at home for a while. It took some getting used to, having a baby in the house. I was glad in the end I'd moved to the room downstairs so I could get some sleep, away from Erica.

We were allowed out at the end of term, to celebrate finishing our exams. It was a proper disco for over eighteens, though no one there was over eighteen. It was just me and Mar again, against the world. We got properly dressed up this time. And Mar had me totally convinced that Leon would be there and we'd get back together and everything would be fine. She didn't think he was weird anymore. At least she didn't say so if she did.

Eoin was there, but she wasn't talking to him. She said she was going to ignore him, though I kept catching her looking at him. There was no sign of Leon. We both of us traipsed around for about the first hour in search of him. Every time we passed Eoin, Mar would look the other way.

Then we sat in a corner, drinking cider through straws we'd brought with us. The first slow set, these boys came up to us, one after the other, asking if we wanted to dance. They were wearing white socks and slip-on black shoes, and all of them seemed to be sporting the same mullet. They'd mutter, 'Dye wanna dance?' then shuffle on to the next girl before you'd even had time to answer, they were that defeated. We were pissed by the second slow set. Eoin came over.

'Howya Mar. Howya Lani,' he said. I didn't hear what went on after that, but she was out on the dance floor with him after about five minutes, and they disappeared out the back for the rest of the night.

Some boy I recognised from Leon's year was staring right at me, so I stared right back. I didn't care because I didn't fancy him.

He came over after a while.

'Were you in Leon Brady's class?' I asked him.

'How did you know?'

'Just.'

'Oh, you must be Lani Devine,' he said. 'I've heard about you.'

'And what have you heard?'

'That you were brave enough to go out with him.'

He could say what he liked. I just wanted to lose myself somehow. Drink wasn't enough.

He sat down beside me and we kissed for a bit. Then he took my hand and we went out the back of the nightclub. I was swaying badly. I couldn't see straight. There were all these couples shoved up against the wall. He dragged me over a barbed-wire fence into a field. I tore the bottom of my jeans. We stumbled behind one of the bales of hay. He grabbed me then and kissed me again. I didn't like the way he kissed. He was like a sucky calf. I kept having to pull his mouth from mine because I didn't like it. He lifted my top up and looked at my breasts. Then he undid his zip and took his dick out of his trousers. All the time he was saying 'God, oh God,' and swaying. He pushed it hard between my legs. I thought he looked so ugly.

I was bored, I didn't want him just slobbering all over me, so I lay down on the grass and pulled him down on top of me, helping him undo the buttons on my jeans and pull them down around my ankles.

He pulled a rubber from his trouser pocket and struggled to put it on, while I lay looking up at the stars. It was all over very quick. I don't remember much about it. It must have hurt, but I don't remember. I just remember his mouth at my ear going 'God, oh God,' because I had my head turned to the side. And the hay scratching my face. He lay down on top of me after, and I couldn't breathe properly. He tried to kiss me again but I turned my head away.

Then he rolled off me and we lay there for ages, my head cradled on his arm, looking up at the sky. Neither of us could think of anything to say. But it was nice, just lying there. I could pretend he was Leon, if I didn't look. And if I didn't smell him, because he smelled different. I breathed through my mouth so I wouldn't have to smell him. I could almost have loved him at that moment, for making me so happy.

Then the earth started heaving under me and I knew that I was going to be sick. I wasn't sick in front of him. Somehow I managed to stumble inside to the toilets. I met Mar at the basins. She wanted to know his name – she'd seen us out the back – but I couldn't remember. I slagged her off for going off with Eoin again. She splashed me with water from the sink.

I felt good after that night. Closer to Leon, somehow.

Near the end of that summer I received a slim bundle of letters in the post – all the letters I had sent Leon. And this:

Dear Lani,

I have lied to you as I have lied to others, because I wanted you to know who I was before knowing what I had experienced. No one seems to want to know. I was there. Sometimes I think that that is where my life began to take shape. In that house. When I was seven years old. I was there. I witnessed my father kill my mother. I can remember nothing from before that time. There: that is me.

I know you won't like that. No one can. And I know that somehow I frighten you. I am, after all, complicit. I didn't try to stop him. I helped to kill her by staying silent. That is why I'm treated the way I am sometimes. That's why people at school look at me funny. Who can blame them?

I don't remember much about my mother. Sometimes I think I remember the smell of her, of her hair. She had fair hair like yours. Her eyes were blue like yours, but I'm not sure if I only know that from looking at photographs. It's so hard to be sure.

She had taken to sleeping in my bed. I was her baby, still. I didn't mind her climbing in beside me each night. I didn't question why she was there. Of course I didn't. I was only a child. They said afterwards that she'd been seeing some man, and my father knew, and that's why they were sleeping separately. But I don't believe that's true. There was never any evidence of that. That was just a dirty rumour.

People said my father had married my mother on the rebound from a local girl he had been with, that he had never really loved my mother. But I don't believe that either. People didn't like her much. They thought she had airs and graces about her. They thought she looked down her nose at them. Just because she was English, probably. She was no different from any of them. They didn't like my father either, after that, though they were probably a little quicker to forgive him.

He read to me that night. I remember that, clear as day. I sat next to him on his favourite chair in the living room. Then he tucked me up in bed. I don't remember my mother being there at all. She must have been in the kitchen cleaning, or upstairs tidying things away. I don't know.

I wasn't woken straight away. I woke up moments too late, when they were in the throes of it, out on the landing. I can't remember exactly. I don't want to. Even if I did I wouldn't want to tell you. It is a private thing.

I think I remember the story being 'Jack and the Beanstalk', and thinking of the giant shouting 'Fee-fi-fo-fum, I smell the blood of an Englishman.' After that I got out of bed. I must have climbed over my own mother's body to get to the stairs. There was no other way I could have gotten out of there. And I do remember standing holding on to the banisters.

The house was dark and quiet after that. All I could hear was Dad on the phone downstairs. I wasn't frightened of him. He had grown into this big fairy-tale giant, but I wasn't scared. I went down and sat on the stairs.

'It's all right now, go back to bed,' he kept saying. I didn't want to walk over my mother again. So I just sat on the steps, shivering. I remember my dad opening the front door, and the guards coming into the house, and turning on every light in every room, and me being taken off to the neighbours, still in my pyjamas. Dad sitting slumped in an armchair in the living room. Pale as a ghost.

I don't remember anyone ever asking me what I saw. It was like I hadn't been there at all. No one wanted to believe that I had been there, and seen what I'd seen. I didn't mind that, but I did mind that everyone else seemed to forget. I had a toy train. I remember showing it to the neighbours. Santa had given it to me.

I was the only witness to my parents' most intimate moment. I have to carry that. No one else wanted to know, wanted to remember. I'm not even sure if Dad does. I've never heard him speak of it.

My aunt came to look after me. She was the only one of

Mam's family who went to the funeral. And someone seems to have decided that it would be too upsetting for me to be there. We never talk about it. I was probably left with the neighbours that day too, though it's all a bit of a blur.

We were in England for a bit, but I don't really remember that very well. I can just vaguely remember the strange school. Sometimes certain things — like particular types of rubbery potted plants or certain mustard colours, even — will remind me of that time. Must have been something to do with the house we were staying in. I get a terrible overwhelming lonely feeling. We moved back into my house then, and even though Dad wasn't there at first it was better than being in a strange place. I didn't move into my old room. That room hasn't been touched since. The same sheets are still on the bed. The door isn't locked or anything, but no one goes in there except to dump things we have no space for. Old boxes for irons and kettles and things. Things we'll never go back to look for.

We changed the carpet on the landing and on the stairs.

I got confused after a while. I started to call my aunt 'Mammy'. I don't think she liked it very much when I did that. But she was good to me. She tried her best to protect me from what people said. But my aunt couldn't love me properly because my father had killed her sister. And my father couldn't love me properly because he had taken my mother away from me, he felt too guilty I suppose.

I don't know how long he was away. He wasn't the same as I remembered when he came back home. He was much more subdued. He wouldn't read me stories anymore. I had to read them myself. But I liked having him around the place. When my aunt went away I was sent off to boarding school. I've been away since. I only see my father the odd time that I'm home. I can't really stand to be there for any length of time. He has his own way of doing things. He's lost in his own thoughts most of the time. It's like I'm in the way.

I felt so sorry for him, though. I still do. I have shared unspeakable things with him. But I love him. He is my father. He is mine and I have no other.

Life paled into insignificance after that night, that moment of intimacy. It all seems so utterly pointless and dreary somehow. I know that probably doesn't make sense. But nothing could ever be as transfiguring as that moment.

Do you see how I cannot trust myself around you? I spied on you. That night when I ran ahead of you and your friend, through the fields, and saw you looking through your bedroom window at your father, it was like seeing myself. And that day when I passed you in the car and couldn't look at you — it was because I was so ashamed of what you knew. That's what I wanted to tell you when I came to find you that night, and what I couldn't say when you came to see me.

I wanted to tell you about things myself, over time. But I was frightened. And it was all taken away from me. I had nothing left.

I can no longer think of you, Lani. I must forget you. I must spend my life forgetting.

Love,
Leon

Acknowledgements

Thank you to Mavis Arnold and Heather Laskey, the authors of *Children of the Poor Clares: The Story of an Irish Orphanage*. Thank you also to my wonderful agents, Tessa David and Caroline Michel at PFD, and to my brilliant editor Jo Dingley (and the whole team at Canongate). And Will – thank you, love, for believing in me.

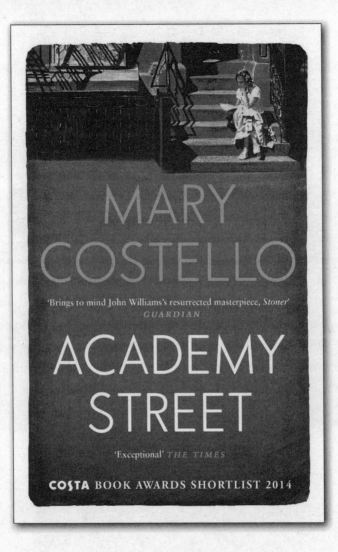

MARY
COSTELLO

'Brings to mind John Williams's resurrected masterpiece, *Stoner*'
GUARDIAN

ACADEMY
STREET

'Exceptional' *THE TIMES*

COSTA BOOK AWARDS SHORTLIST 2014

'Packed with emotional intensity'
Sunday Times

CANON▊GATE

'Books like this come along once in a generation' *New York Times*

CANON■GATE

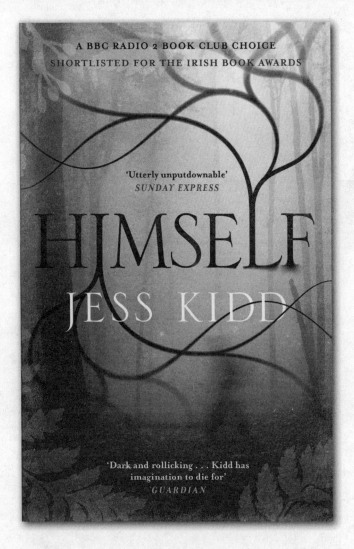

A BBC RADIO 2 BOOK CLUB CHOICE
SHORTLISTED FOR THE IRISH BOOK AWARDS

'Utterly unputdownable'
SUNDAY EXPRESS

HIMSELF

JESS KIDD

'Dark and rollicking . . . Kidd has
imagination to die for'
GUARDIAN

'Otherwordly and wonderfully original'
Stylist

CANON‖GATE